RUSKIN BOND
The Beast with Five Fingers

Ruskin Bond has been writing for over sixty years, and now has over 120 titles in print—novels, collections of short stories, poetry, essays, anthologies and books for children. His first novel, *The Room on the Roof*, received the prestigious John Llewellyn Rhys Prize in 1957. He has also received the Padma Shri (1999), the Padma Bhushan (2014) and two awards from Sahitya Akademi—one for his short stories and another for his writings for children. In 2012, the Delhi government gave him its Lifetime Achievement Award.

Born in 1934, Ruskin Bond grew up in Jamnagar, Shimla, New Delhi and Dehradun. Apart from three years in the UK, he has spent all his life in India, and now lives in Mussoorie with his adopted family.

RUSKIN BOND
The Beast with Five Fingers

Edited & Compiled by
RUSKIN BOND

Published by
Rupa Publications India Pvt. Ltd 2018
161-B/4, Gulmohar House,
Yusuf Sarai Community Centre,
New Delhi 110049

Sales centres:
Bengaluru Chennai
Hyderabad Kolkata Mumbai

Copyright © Ruskin Bond 2018

This is a work of fiction. Names, characters, places and incidents are either the product of the author's imagination or are used fictiously and any resemblance to any actual person, living or dead, events or locales is entirely coincidental.

All rights reserved.
No part of this publication may be reproduced, transmitted, or stored in a retrieval system, in any form or by any means, electronic, mechanical, photocopying, recording or otherwise, without the prior permission of the publisher.

P-ISBN: 978-81-291-5078-3
E-ISBN: 978-81-291-5079-0

Twelfth impression 2026

15 14 13 12

The moral right of the author has been asserted.

Printed in India

This book is sold subject to the condition that it shall not, by way of trade or otherwise, be lent, resold, hired out, or otherwise circulated, without the publisher's prior consent, in any form of binding or cover other than that in which it is published.

CONTENTS

Introduction	vii
Florence Flannery *Marjorie Bowen*	1
The Hollow Man *Thomas Burke*	24
The Doctor's Ghost *Dr Norman Macleod*	40
The Phantom 'Rickshaw *Rudyard Kipling*	46
Night of the Millennium *Ruskin Bond*	73
The Mirror *Reeta Dutta Gupta*	76
The Beast with Five Fingers *W.F. Harvey*	86
Boomerang *Oscar Cook*	118

INTRODUCTION

If you have enjoyed the ghost stories compiled by me earlier then will you will find the collection of horror stories in this volume just as spooky. A terrifying mix of remote bungalows, jackals, cemeteries, a ghostly human hand, and haunted mirrors—these grisly tales of phantoms and beasts will not disappoint any horror fan.

Are ghosts real? I for one haven't been able to find the answer. But what I have realized over the years is that fear is real. I have myself have felt scared to the bones on several occasions, sometimes even just because of an ivy branch tapping at my window at night.

This is a collection of some classic tales, period chillers, written by masters of the macabre—Marjorie Bowen, Rudyard Kipling, W.F. Harvey, Oscar Cook, and others—as well as a few lesser-known hair-raisers from across the world. From haunted rickshaws and the walking dead to stories of human and animal ferocity—these are supernatural tales that will chill the blood.

Phantoms don't always come after you when you are asleep in your warm bed. It can also fancy the outdoors—lurking behind the trees while you are out on your evening walk alone. Take care, because terror lurks where you least expect it.

This book is for long winter evenings of drawn curtains

and dim lights. For when the moonlight streams through the window and the jackal howls, horror and adventure will not be contained in the pages of these spooky stories!

Ruskin Bond

FLORENCE FLANNERY

By Marjorie Bowen

She who had been Florence Flannery noted with a careless eye the stains of wet on the dusty stairs, and with a glance ill used to observance of domesticities looked up for damp or dripping ceilings. The dim-walled staircase revealed nothing but more dust, yet this would serve as a peg for ill-humour to hang on, so Florence pouted.

'An ill, muddy place,' said she, who loved gilding and gimcracks and mirrors reflecting velvet chairs, and flounced away to the upper chamber, lifting frilled skirts contemptuously high.

Her husband followed; they had been married a week and there had never been any happiness in their wilful passion. Daniel Shute did not now look for any; in the disgust of this draggled homecoming he wondered what had induced him to marry the woman and how soon he would come to hate her.

As she stood in the big bedroom he watched her with dislike; her tawdry charms of vulgar prettiness had once been delightful to his dazed senses and muddled wits, but here, in his old home, washed by the fine Devon air, his sight was clearer and she appeared coarse as a poppy at the far end of August.

'Of course you hate it,' he said cynically, lounging with his big shoulders against one of the bedposts, his big hands in the pockets of his tight nankeen trousers, and his fair hair, tousled from the journey, hanging over his mottled face.

'It is not the place you boasted to have,' replied Florence, but idly, for she stood by the window and looked at the tiny leaded panes; the autumn sun gleaming sideways on this glass, picked out a name scratched there:

Florence Flannery. Born 1500.

'Look here,' cried the woman, excited, 'this should be my ancestress!'

She slipped off a huge diamond ring she wore and scratched underneath the writing the present year, '1800'.

Daniel Shute came and looked over her shoulder.

'That reads strange—"Born 1500"—as if you would say died 1800,' he remarked. 'Well, I don't suppose she had anything to do with you, my charmer, yet she brought you luck, for it was remembering this name here made me notice you when I heard what you were called.'

He spoke uncivilly, and she responded in the same tone.

'Undervalue what is your own, Mr Shute. There was enough for me to choose from, I can swear!'

'Enough likely gallants,' he grinned, 'not so many likely husbands, eh?'

He slouched away, for, fallen as he was, it stung him that he had married a corybant of the opera, an unplaced, homeless nameless creature for all he knew, for he could never quite believe that 'Florence Flannery' was her real name.

Yet that name had always attracted him; it was so queer that he should meet a real woman called Florence Flannery when one of the earliest of his recollections was tracing that name over with a curious finger in the old diamond pane.

'You have never told me who she was,' said Mrs Shute.

'Who knows? Three hundred years ago, m'dear. There are some old wives' tales, of course.'

He left the great bedroom and she followed him doggedly downstairs.

'Is this your fine manor, Mr Shute? And these your noble grounds? And how am I to live here, Mr Shute, who left the gaieties of London for you?'

Her voice, shrill and edged, followed him down the stairs and into the vast dismantled drawing-room where they paused, facing each other like things caught in a trap, which is what they were.

For he had married her because he was a ruined man, driven from London by duns, and a drunken man who dreaded lonely hours and needed a boon companion to pledge him glass for glass, and a man of coarse desires who had bought with marriage what he was not rich enough to buy with money, and she had married him because she was past her meridian and saw no more conquests ahead and also was in love with the idea of being a gentlewoman and ruling in the great grand house by the sea—which was how she had thought of Shute Manor.

And a great grand house it had been, but for twenty years it had been abandoned by Daniel Shute, and stripped and mortgaged to pay for his vices, so that now it stood barren and desolate, empty and tarnished, and only a woman with love in her heart could have made a home of it; never had there been love in Florence Flannery's heart, only greed and meanness.

Thus, these two faced each other in the gaunt room with the monstrous chandelier hanging above them wrapped in a dusty brown holland bag, the walls festooned with cobwebs, the pale wintry sunshine showing the thick dust on the unpolished boards.

'I never can live here!' cried Mrs Shute. There was a touch of panic in her voice and she lifted her hands to her heart with a womanly gesture of grief.

The man was touched by a throb of pity; he did not himself expect the place to be so dilapidated. Some kind of a rascally agent had been looking after it for him, and he supposed some effort would have been made for his reception.

Florence saw his look of half-sullen shame and urged her point.

'We can go back, cannot we?' she said, with the rich drop in her voice, so useful for coaxing; 'back to London and the house in Baker Street? All the old friends and old pleasures, Mr Shute, and a dashing little cabriolet to go round the park?'

'Curse it!' he answered, chagrined. 'I haven't the money, Flo; I haven't the damned money!' She heard the ring of bitter truth in his voice and the atrocious nature of the deception he had practised on her overwhelmed her shallow understanding.

'You mean you've got no money, Mr Shute?' she screamed.

'Not enough for London, m'dear.'

'And I've to live in this filthy barn?'

'It has been good enough for my people, Mrs Shute,' he answered grimly. 'For all the women of my family, gentlewomen, all of 'em with quarterings, and it will be good enough for you, m'dear, so none of your Bartholomew Fair airs and graces.'

She was cornered, and a little afraid of him; he had been drinking at the last place where they stopped to water the horses and she knew how he could be when he was drunk; she remembered that she was alone with him and what a huge man he was.

So she crept away and went down into the vast kitchens where an old woman and a girl were preparing a meal.

The sight of this a little heartened Mrs Shute; in her frilled taffetas and long ringlets she sat down by the great open hearth, moving her hands to show the firelight flashing in her rings and shifting her petticoats so that the girl might admire her kid shoes.

'I'll take a cordial to stay my strength,' she said, 'for I've come a long way and find a sour welcome at the end of it, and that'll turn any woman's blood.'

The old dame smiled, knowing her type well enough; for even in a village you may find women like this.

So she brought Mrs Shute some damson wine and a plate of biscuits, and the two women became friendly enough and gossiped in the dim candle-lit kitchen while Daniel Shute wandered about his old home, even his corrupt heart feeling many a pang to see the places of his childhood desolate, the walks overgrown, the trees felled, the arbours closed, the fountains dried, and all the spreading fields about fenced by strangers.

The November moon was high in a misted space of open heaven by the time he reached the old carp pond.

Dead weeds tangled over the crumbling, moss-grown stone, trumpery and slime coated the dark waters.

'I suppose the carp are all dead?' said Mr Shute. He had not been aware that he spoke aloud, and was surprised to hear himself answered.

'I believe there are some left, esquire.'

Mr Shute turned sharply and could faintly discern the figure of a man sitting on the edge of the pond so that it seemed as if his legs half-dangled in the black water.

'Who are you?' asked Daniel Shute quickly.

'I'm Paley, sir, who looks after the grounds.'

'You do your work damned badly,' replied the other, irritated.

'It is a big place, esquire, for one man to work.'

He seemed to stoop lower and lower as if at any moment he would slip into the pond; indeed, in the half-dark, it seemed to Mr Shute as if he was already half in the water; yet, on this speech, he moved and showed that he was but bending over the sombre depths of the carp pond.

The moonlight displayed him as a drab man of middling proportions with slow movements and a large languid eye which glittered feebly in the pale light; Mr Shute had an impression that this eye looked at him sideways as if it was set at the side of the man's head, but soon saw that this was an illusion.

'Who engaged you?' he asked acidly, hating the creature.

'Mr Tregaskis, the agent,' replied the man in what appeared to be a thick foreign accent or with some defect of speech, and walked away into the wintry undergrowth.

Mr Shute returned home grumbling; in the grim parlour Mr Tregaskis was waiting for him—a red Cornishman, who grinned at his employer's railings. He knew the vices of Mr Shute, and the difficulties of Mr Shute, and he had seen Mrs Shute in the kitchen deep in maudlin gossip with old Dame Chase and the idiot-faced girl, drinking the alcoholic country wine till it spilled from her shaking fingers on to her taffeta skirt.

So, he assumed a tone of noisy familiarity that Mr Shute was too sunken to resent; the last of the old squire's Oporto was sent for and the men drank themselves on to terms of easy good-fellowship.

At the last, when the candles were guttering, the bottles empty, and the last log's ashes on the hearth, Mr Shute asked who was the creature Paley he had found hanging over the carp pond.

Mr Tregaskis told him, but the next morning Mr Shute could not recollect what he had said; the whole evening had, in his recollection, an atmosphere of phantasmagoria; but he thought that the agent had said that Paley was a deserted sailor who had wandered up from Plymouth and taken the work without pay, a peculiar individual who lived in a wattled hut that he had made himself, and on food he caught with his own hands.

His sole explanation of himself was that he had waited for something a long time and was still waiting for it; useful he was, Mr Tregaskis had said, and it was better to leave him alone.

All this Mr Shute remembered vaguely, lying in the great bed staring at the pale sun glittering on the name 'Florence Flannery' scratched on the window with the two dates.

It was late in the autumnal morning, but his wife still lay beside him, heavily asleep, with her thick heavy chestnut hair tossed over the pillow and her full bosom panting, the carnation of her rounded face flushed and stained, the coarse diamonds glowing on her plump hands, the false pearls slipping round her curved throat.

Daniel Shute sat up in bed and looked down at her prone sleep.

'Who is she? And where does she come from?' he wondered. He had never cared to find out, but now his ignorance of all appertaining to his wife annoyed him.

He shook her bare shoulder till she yawned out of her heavy sleep.

'Who are you, Flo?' he asked. 'You must know something about yourself.'

The woman blinked up at him, drawing her satin bedgown round her breast.

'I was in the opera, wasn't I?' she answered lazily. 'I never knew my people.'

'Came out of an orphanage or the gutter, I suppose?' he returned bitterly.

'Maybe.'

'But your name?' he insisted. 'That is never your name, "Florence Flannery"?'

'I've never known another,' she responded indifferently.

'You're not Irish.'

'I don't know, Mr Shute. I've been in many countries and seen many strange things.'

He laughed; he had heard some of her experiences.

'You've seen so much and been in so many places I don't know how you've ever got it all into one life.'

'I don't know myself It's all rather like a dream and the most dreamlike of all is to be lying here looking at my own name written three hundred years ago.'

She moved restlessly and slipped from the bed, a handsome woman with troubled eyes.

'"Tis the drink brings the dreams, m'dear,' said Mr Shute. 'I had some dreams last night of a fellow named Paley I met by the carp pond.'

'You were drinking in the parlour,' she retorted scornfully.

'And you in the kitchen, m'dear.'

Mrs Shute flung a fringed silk shawl, the gift of an Indian nabob, round her warm body and dropped, shivering and yawning, into one of the warm tapestry chairs.

'Who was this Florence Flannery?' she asked idly.

'I told you no one knows. An Irish girl born in Florence, they said, when I was a child and listened to beldam's gossip. Her mother a Medici, m'dear, and he a groom! And she came here, the trollop, with some young Shute who had been travelling in Italy—picked her up and brought her home, like I've brought you!'

'He didn't marry her?' asked Mrs Shute indifferently.

'More sense,' said her husband coarsely. 'I'm the first fool of me family. She was a proper vixen. John Shute took her on his voyages; he'd a ship and went discovering. They talk yet at Plymouth of how she would sit among the parrots and the spices and the silks when the ship came into Plymouth Hoe.'

'Ah, the good times!' sighed Mrs Shute, 'when men were men and paid a good price for their pleasures!'

'You've fetched your full market value, Mrs Shute,' he answered, yawning in the big bed.

'I'd rather be John Shute's woman than your wife,' she returned.

'What do you know of him?'

'I saw his portrait on the back stairs last night. Goody Chase showed me. A noble man with a clear eye and great arms to fight and love with.'

'He used 'em to push Florence Flannery out with,' grinned Mr Shute, 'if half the tales are true. On one of their voyages they picked up a young Portuguese who took the lady's fancy and she brought him back to Shute Court.'

'And what was the end of it?'

'I know no more, save that she was flung out, as I'd like to fling you out, my beauty!' foamed Mr Shute with gusty violence.

His wife laughed loud and discordantly.

'I'll tell the rest of the tale. She got tired of her new love, and he wasn't a Portuguese, but an Indian, or partly, and his name was D'Ailey, Daly the people called it here. On one voyage she told John Shute about him and he marooned him on a lonely island in the South Seas—tied up to a great, great stone image of a god, burning hot in the tropic sun. He must have been a god of fishes for there was nothing else near that island but monstrous fish.'

'Who told you this?' demanded Mr Shute. 'Old Dame Chase, with her lies? I never heard of this before.'

"'Tis the story,' resumed his wife. 'The last she saw of him was his bound figure tied tight, tight, to the gaping, grinning idol while she sat on the poop as the ship—the *Phoenix*—sailed away. He cursed her and called on the idol to let her live till he was avenged on her—he was of the breed, or partly of the breed, that these gods love, and Florence Flannery was afraid, afraid, as she sailed away—'

'Goody Chase in her cups!' sneered Mr Shute. 'And what's the end of your story?'

'There's no end,' said the woman sullenly. 'John Shute cast her off, for the bad luck that clogged him, and what became of her I don't know.'

'It's an ugly tale and a stupid tale,' grumbled Daniel Shute with a groan as he surveyed the bleak chill weather beyond the lattice panes. 'Get down and see what's to eat in the house and what's to drink in the cellar, and if that rogue Tregaskis is there send him up to me.'

Mrs Shute rose and pulled fiercely at the long wool-embroidered bell-rope so that the rusty bell jangled violently.

'What'll you do when the wine is all drunk and the boon companions have cleared out your pockets?' she asked wildly. 'Do your own errands, Mr Shute.'

He flung out of bed with a pretty London oath, and she remained huddled in the chair while he dressed and after he had left her, wringing her hands now and then and wailing under her breath, till Dame Chase came up with a posset and helped her to dress. The sight of her dishevelled trunks restored some of Mrs Shute's spirits; she pulled out with relish her furbelows and flounces, displaying to Goody Chase's amazed admiration the last fashions of Paris and London, mingling her display with fond reminiscences of gilded triumphs.

'Maybe you'd be surprised to learn that Mr Shute isn't my

first husband,' she said, tossing her head.

The fat old woman winked.

'I'd be more surprised, m'lady, to learn he was your last.'

Mrs Shute laughed grossly, but her spirits soon fell; kneeling on the floor with her tumbled finery in her lap, she stared out through the window on which her name was written at the tossing bare boughs, the chill sky, the dry flutter of the last leaves.

'I'll never get away,' she said mournfully, 'the place bodes me no good. I've had the malaria in me time, Mrs Chase, in one of those cursed Italian swamps and it affected me memory; there's much I can't place together and much I recall brokenly—dreams and fevers, Mrs Chase.'

'The drink, m'lady.'

'No,' returned the kneeling woman fiercely. 'Wasn't the drink taken to drown those dreams and fevers? I wish I could tell you half I know—there's many a fine tale in me head, but when I begin to speak it goes!'

She began to rock to and fro, lamenting.

'To think of the fine times I've had with likely young men drinking me health in me slipper and the little cabriolet in Paris and the walks in the Prater outside Vienna. So pleasant you would hardly believe!'

'You'll settle down, m'lady, like women do.'

Indeed, Mrs Shute seemed to make some attempt at 'settling down'; there was something piteous in the despairing energy with which she set to work to make her life tolerable; there was a suite of rooms lined with faded watered green silk that she took for her own and had cleaned and furnished with what she could gather from the rest of the house—old gilt commodes and rococo chairs and threadbare panels of tapestries and chipped vases of Saxe or Luneville, one or two pastel portraits that the damp had stained together with some tawdry trifles she had brought in her own baggage.

She employed Mr Tregaskis to sell her big diamond in Plymouth and bought pale blue satin hangings for her bedroom and spotted muslin for her bed, a carpet wreathed with roses, a gaudy dressing-table and phials of perfume, opopanax, frangipane, musk, potent, searing, to dissipate, she said, the odours of must and mildew.

Arranging these crude splendours was her sole occupation. There were no neighbours in the lonely valley and Mr Shute fell into melancholy and solitary drinking; he hung on to this existence as just more tolerable than a debtor's prison, but the fury with which he met his fate expressed itself in curses awful to hear. Such part of the estate as still belonged to him he treated with complex contempt; Mr Tregaskis continued to supervise some rough farming and the man, Paley, worked in the garden; taciturn, solitary and sullen, he made an ill impression on Mr Shute, yet he cost nothing and did some labour, as carrying up the firewood to the house and clearing away some of the thickets and dying weeds and vast clumps of nettles and docks.

Mrs Shute met him for the first time by the carp pond; she was tricked out in a white satin pelisse edged with fur and a big bonnet, and wandered forlornly in the neglected paths. Paley was sitting on the edge of the carp pond, looking intently into the murky depths.

'I'm the new mistress,' said Mrs Shute, 'and I'll thank you to keep better order in the place.'

Paley looked up at her with his pale eyes.

'Shute Court isn't what it was,' he said, 'there is a lot of work to do.'

'You seem to spend a power of time by the pond,' she replied. 'What are you here for?'

'I'm waiting for something,' he said. 'I'm putting in time,

Mrs Shute.'

'A sailor, I hear?' she said curiously, for the draggled nondescript man in his greenish-black clothes was difficult to place; he had a peculiar look of being boneless, without shoulders or hips, one slope slipping into another as if there was no framework under his flabby flesh.

'I've been at sea,' he answered, 'like yourself, Mrs Shute.'

She laughed coarsely.

'I would like if I were at sea again,' she replied; 'this is horror to me.'

'Why do you stay?'

'I'm wondering. It seems that I can't get away, the same as I couldn't help coming,' a wail came into her voice. 'Must I wait till Mr Shute has drunk himself to death?'

The wind blew sharp across the pond, cutting little waver, in the placid surface, and she who had been Florence Flannery shuddered in the bite of it and turned away and went muttering up the path to the desolate house.

Her husband was in the dirty parlour playing at bezique with Mr Tregaskis and she flared in upon them.

'Why don't you get rid of that man Paley? I hate him. He does no work—Mrs Chase told me that he always sits by the carp pond and today I saw him—ugh!'

'Paley's all right, Mrs Shute,' replied Tregaskis, 'he does more work than you think.'

'Why does he stay?'

'He's waiting for a ship that's soon due in Plymouth.'

'Send him off,' insisted Mrs Shute. 'Isn't the place melancholic enough without you having that sitting about?'

Her distaste and disgust of the man seemed to amount to a panic, and her husband, whose courage was snapped by the drink, was infected by her fear.

'When did this fellow come?' he demanded.

About a week before you did. He'd tramped up from Plymouth.'

'We've only his word for that,' replied Mr Shute with drunken cunning; 'maybe he's a Bow Street runner sent by one of those damned creditors! You're right, Flo, I don't like the wretch—he's watching me, split him! I'll send him off.'

Mr Tregaskis shrugged as Daniel Shute staggered from his chair.

'The man's harmless, sir; half-witted if you like, but useful.'

Still Mr Shute dragged on his greatcoat with the capes and followed his wife out into the grey garden.

The carp pond was not near the house, and by the time that they had reached it a dull twilight had fallen in the cold heavy air.

The great trees were quite bare now and flung a black tracing of forlorn branches against the bleak evening sky; patches and clumps of dead weeds obstructed every path and alley; by the carp pond showed the faint outline of a blind statue crumbling beneath the weight of dead mosses.

Paley was not there.

'He'll be in his hut,' said Mr Shute, 'sleeping or spying—the ugly old devil. I'll send him off.'

The dead oyster white of Mrs Shute's pelisse gleamed oddly as she followed her husband through the crackling undergrowth.

There, in the thickening twilight, they found the hut, a queer arrangement of wattles cunningly interwoven in which there was no furniture whatever, nothing but a bare protection from the wind and weather.

Paley was not there.

''Til I find him,' muttered Mr Shute, 'if I have to stay out all night.'

For his half-intoxicated mind had fixed on this stranger as the symbol of all his misfortunes and perhaps the avenger of all his vices.

His wife turned back, for her pelisse was being caught on the undergrowth; she went moodily towards the carp pond.

A moment later a sharp shriek from her brought Mr Shute plunging back to her side. She was standing in a queer bent attitude, pointing with a shaking plump hand to the murky depths of the pond.

'The wretch! He's drowned himself!' she screamed.

Mr Shute's worn-out nerves reacted to her ignoble panic; he clutched her arm as he gazed in the direction of her finger; there was something dark in the shallower side of the pond, something large and dark, with pale flat eyes that glittered malevolently.

'Paley!' gasped Mr Shute.

He bent closer in amazed horror, then broke into tremulous laughter.

"Tis a fish,' he declared; 'one of the old carp.'

Mrs Shute indeed now perceived that the monstrous creature in the water was a fish; she could make out the wide gaping jaw tall spines shadowing in the murk, and a mottled skin of deadly yellow and dingy white.

'It's looking at me,' she gasped. 'Kill it, kill it, the loathsome wretch!'

'It's—it's—too big,' stammered Mr Shute, but he picked up a stone to hurl; the huge fish, as if aware of his intentions, slipped away into the murky depths of the pond, leavings sluggish ripple on the surface.

Daniel Shute now found his courage.

'Nothing but an old carp,' he repeated. 'I'll have the thing caught.'

Mrs Shute began to weep and wring her hands. Her husband

dragged her roughly towards the house, left her there, took a lantern, and accompanied now by Mr Tregaskis returned in search of Paley.

This time they found him sitting in his usual place by the side of the pond. Mr Shute had now changed his mind about sending him away; he had a muddled idea that he would like the pond watched, and who was to do this if not Paley?

'Look here, my man,' he said, 'there's a great carp in this pond—a very big, black old carp.'

'They live for hundreds of years,' said Paley. 'But this isn't a carp.'

'You know about it, then?' demanded Mr Shute.

'I know about it.'

'Well, I want you to catch it—kill it. Watch till you do. I loathe it—ugh!'

'Watch the pond?' protested Mr Tregaskis, who held the lantern and was chilled and irritable. 'Damme, esquire, what can the thing do? It can't leave the water.'

'I wouldn't,' muttered Mr Shute, 'promise you that.'

'You're drunk,' said the other coarsely.

But Mr Shute insisted on his point.

'Watch the pond, Paley, watch it day and night till you get that fish.'

'I'll watch,' answered Paley, never moving from his huddled position.

The two men went back to the desolate house. When Mr Shute at last staggered upstairs he found his wife with half a dozen candles lit, crouching under the tawdry muslin curtains with which she had disfigured the big bed.

She clutched a rosary that she was constantly raising to her lips as she muttered ejaculations.

Mr Shute lurched to the bedside.

'I didn't know that you were a Papist, Flo,' he sneered.

She looked up at him.

'That story's got me,' she whispered, 'the man tied up to the fish god—the curse—and he following her—tracking her down—for three hundred years, till she was hounded back to the old place where they'd loved.'

Daniel Shute perceived that she had been drinking, and sank into a chair.

'Goody Chase's gossip,' he answered, yawning, 'and that damned ugly fish. I've set Paley to catch him—to watch the pond till he does.'

She looked at him sharply, and appeared relieved.

'Anyhow, what's it to do with you?' he continued. 'You ain't the jade who left the man on the island!' He laughed crudely.

Mrs Shute sank down on her pillows.

'As long as the pond is watched,' she murmured, 'I don't mind.'

But during the night she tossed and panted in a delirium talking of great ships with strange merchandise, of lonely islands amid blazing seas, of mighty stone gods rearing up to the heavens of a man in torture and a curse following a woman who sailed away, till her husband shook her and left her alone, sleeping on a couch in the dreary parlour.

The next day he spoke to Mrs Chase.

'Between your news and your lies you've turned your mistress's head. Good God! she is like a maniac with your parcel of follies!'

But Goody Chase protested that she had told her nothing.

'She told me that story, esquire, and said she had found it in an old book. What did I know of Florence Flannery? Many a time you've asked me about her when you were a child and I've had no answer to give you—what did I know save she was a hussy who disgraced Shute Court?'

At this Daniel Shute vehemently demanded of his wife where she had got the tales which she babbled about, but the woman was sullen and heavy and would tell him nothing; all the day she remained thus, but when the few hours of wintry light were over she fell again into unbridled terror, gibbering like a creature deprived of reason, beating her breast, kissing the rosary, and muttering, *'Mea culpâ mea culpâ, mea maximâ culpâ!'*

Mr Shute was not himself in any state to endure this; he left his wife to herself and made Tregaskis sleep with him for company in another room.

Winter froze the bleak countryside; Paley kept guard by the pond and the Shutes somehow dragged on an intolerable existence in the deserted house.

In the daytime Mrs Shute revived a little and would even prink herself out in her finery and gossip with Mrs Chase over the vast log fire, but the nights always found her smitten with terror, shivering with cowardly apprehension; and the object of all her nightmare dread was the fish she had seen in the pond.

'It can't leave the water,' they told her, and she always answered:

'The first night I was here I saw wet on the stairs.'

'My God, my God!' Daniel Shute would say, 'this is like living with some one sentenced to death.'

'Get a doctor over from Plymouth,' suggested Mr Tregaskis.

But Mr Shute would not, for fear of being betrayed to his creditors.

'Better rot here than in the Fleet,' he swore.

'Then take her away—and keep her from the bottle.'

The wretched husband could do neither of these things; he had no money and no influence over Mrs Shute. He was indeed indifferent to her sufferings save in so far as they reacted on him and ever accustomed him to the spectacle of her breakdown; he knew it was not really strange that a woman such as she was should collapse under conditions such as these, and his life was already so wretched that he cared little for added horrors.

He began to find a strange comfort in the man Paley, who taciturn, slow and queer, yet did his work and watched the pond with an admirable diligence.

One night in the blackest time of the year, the bitter dark nights before Christmas, the shrieks of Mrs Shute brought her husband cursing up the stairs.

Her door was unbolted and she sat up in bed, displaying, in the light of his snatched-up taper, some red marks on her arm.

'Let him kill me and be done with it,' she jabbered.

Mr Tregaskis came pushing in and caught rudely hold of her arm.

'She's done it herself,' he cried; 'those are the marks of her own teeth.'

But Mrs Shute cried piteously:

'He came flopping up the stairs, he broke the bolts; he jumped on the bed! Oh! oh! oh! Isn't this the bed, the very bed I slept in then—and didn't he used to creep into this room when John Shute was away?'

'Still thinking of that damned fish,' said Mr Tregaskis, 'and it's my belief you neither of you saw it at all, esquire—that man Paley has been watching, and he's seen nothing.'

Mr Shute bit his finger-nails, looking down on the writhing figure of his wife.

'Light all the candles, can't you?' he said. 'I'll stay with the poor fool tonight.'

While Mr Tregaskis obeyed he went to the door and looked out, holding his taper high.

There were pools of wet and a long trail of slime down

the dusty, neglected stairs.

He called Mr Tregaskis.

'Ugh!' cried the Cornishman, then. 'It's from Goody Chase's water crock.'

On the following windy morning Mr Shute went out, shivering in the nipping air, to the carp pond.

'I don't want another night like last,' he said. 'You'll sleep across my wife's door—she thinks that cursed carp is after her—'

Then, at the gross absurdity of what he said, he laughed miserably.

'This is a pretty pantomime I'm playing,' he muttered.

A horrid curiosity drove him up to look at his wife.

She sat between the draggled muslin curtains hugging her knees in the tumbled bed; a wretched fire flickered wanly in the chill depths of the vast room; a wind blew swift and remote round the window on which was scratched the name of Florence Flannery.

Mr Shute shivered.

'I must get you away,' he said, stirred above his fears for himself; 'this is a damned place—the Fleet would be better, after all.'

She turned lustreless eyes on him.

'I can't get away,' she said dully. 'I've come here to die—don't you see it on that window—"Died 1800?"'

He crossed the floor and peered at the scratching on the glass. Some one had indeed added the word 'died' before the last date.

'These are the tricks of a Bedlamite,' he said nervously. 'Do you think there was only one Florence Flannery?'

'And do you think,' she returned harshly, 'that there were two?'

She looked so awful crouched up in bed with her hanging

hair, her once plump face fallen in the cheeks, her soiled satin gown open over her labouring breast, her whole air and expression so agonized, so malevolent, so dreadful, that Daniel Shute passed his hand over his eyes as if to brush away a vision of unsubstantial horror.

He was shaken by a hallucination of light-headedness; he appeared to enter another world, in which many queer things were possible.

'What are you?' he asked uneasily. 'He's been after you for nearly three hundred years? Aren't you punished enough?'

'Oh, oh!' moaned the woman. 'Keep him out! Keep him out!'

'I'll put Paley at the door tonight,' muttered Mr Shute.

He crept out of the horrible chamber; he now detested his wife beyond all reason, yet somehow he felt impelled to save her from the invincible furies who were pursuing her in so gruesome a fashion.

'She's a lunatic,' said Mr Tregaskis brusquely. 'You'll have to keep her shut up in that room—it's not difficult to account for—with the life she's led and this place and the coincidence of the names.'

The first snow of the year began to fall that night, sullen flakes struggling in the coils of the leaping wind that circled round Shute Court.

In the last glimmer of daylight Paley came to take up his post.

Drab, silent, with his sloping shoulders and nondescript clothes, he went slowly upstairs and sat down outside Mrs Shute's door.

'He seems to know the way,' remarked Daniel Shute.

'Don't you know he works in the house?' retorted Mr Tregaskis.

The two men slept, as usual, in the parlour, on stiff horsehair couches bundled up with pillows and blankets; the litter of their supper was left on the table and they piled the fire up with logs before going to sleep. Mr Shute's nerves were in no state to permit him to risk waking up in the dark.

The wind dropped and the steady downdrift of the soft snow filled the blackness of the bitter night.

As the grandfather clock struck three Daniel Shute sat up and called to his companion.

'I've been thinking in my dreams,' he said, with chattering teeth. 'Is it Paley, or Daley? You know the name was D'Ailey.'

'Shut up, you fool,' returned the agent fiercely; but he then raised himself on his elbow for a hoarse, bitter scream, followed by some yelled words in a foreign language tore through the stillness.

'The mad woman,' said Mr Tregaskis; but Daniel Shute dragged the clothes up to his chattering teeth.

'I'm not going up,' he muttered. 'I'm not going up!'

Mr Tregaskis dragged on his trousers and flung a blanket over his shoulders and so, lighting a taper at the big fire, went up the gaunt stairs to Mrs Shute's room. The glimmering reams of the rushlight showed him tracks of wet again on the dirty boards.

'Goody Chase with her crocks and possets,' he murmured; then louder, 'Paley! Paley!'

There was no one outside Mrs Shute's door, which hung open. Mr Tregaskis entered.

She who had been Florence Flannery lay prone on her tawdry couch; the deep wounds that had slain her appeared to have been torn by savage teeth: she looked infinitely old, shrivelled and detestable.

Mr Tregaskis backed on to the stairs, the light lurching round him from the shaking of his taper, when Mr Shute came bustling up out of the darkness.

'Paley's gone,' whispered Mr Tregaskis dully.

'I saw him go,' gibbered Mr Shute, 'as I ventured to the door—by the firelight; a great fish slithering away with blood on his jaws.'

THE HOLLOW MAN

Thomas Burke

He came up one of the narrow streets which lead from the docks, and turned into a road whose farther end was gay with the light of London. At the end of this road he went deep into the lights of London, and sometimes into its shadows, farther and farther away from the river; and did not pause until he had reached a poor quarter near the centre.

He was a tall, spare figure, wearing a black mackintosh. Below this could be seen brown dungaree trousers. A peaked cap hid most of his face; the little that was exposed was white and sharp. In the autumn mist that filled the lighted streets, as well as the dark, he seemed a wraith; and some of those who passed him looked again, not sure whether they had indeed seen a living man. One or two of them moved their shoulders, as though shrinking from something.

His legs were long, but he walked with the short, deliberate steps of a blind man, though he was not blind. His eyes were open, and he stared straight ahead; but he seemed to see nothing and hear nothing.

Neither the mournful hooting of sirens across the black water of the river nor the genial windows of the shops in the big streets near the centre drew his head to the right or left. He walked as though he had no destination in mind, yet constantly, at this corner or that, he turned. It seemed that an unseen hand was guiding him to a given point, of whose location he was himself ignorant.

He was searching for a friend of fifteen years ago, and the unseen hand, or some dog-instinct, had led him from Africa to London, and was now leading him, along the last mile of his search, to a certain little eating-house. He did not know that he was going to the eating-house of his friend Nameless, but he did know, from the time he left Africa, that he was journeying towards Nameless, and he now knew that he was very near to Nameless.

Nameless didn't know that his old friend was anywhere near him, though, had he observed the conditions that evening, he might have wondered why he was sitting up an hour later than usual. He was seated in one of the pews of his prosperous little workmen's dining-rooms—a little gold-mine his wife's relations called it—and he was smoking and looking at nothing.

He had added up the till and written the copies of the bill of fare for next day, and there was nothing to keep him out of bed after his fifteen hours' attention to business. Had he been asked why he was sitting up later than usual, he would first have answered that he didn't know that he was, and would then have explained, in default of any other explanation, that it was for the purpose of having a last pipe. He was quite unaware that he was sitting up and keeping the door unlatched because a long-parted friend from Africa was seeking him and slowly approaching him, and needed his services.

He was quite unaware that he had left the door unlatched at that late hour—half-past eleven—to admit pain and woe.

But even as many bells sent dolefully across the night from

their steeples their disagreement as to the point of half-past eleven, pain and woe were but two streets away from him. The mackintosh and dungarees and the sharp white face were coming nearer every moment.

There was silence in the house and in the streets; a heavy silence, broken, or sometimes stressed, by the occasional night-noises—motor horns, back-firing of lorries, shunting at a distant terminus. That silence seemed to envelop the house, but he did not notice it. He did not notice the bells, and he did not even notice the lagging step that approached his shop, and passed— and returned—and passed again—and halted. He was aware of nothing save that he was smoking a last pipe, and he was sitting in that state of hazy reverie which he called thinking, deaf and blind to anything not in his immediate neighbourhood.

But when a hand was laid on the latch, and the latch was lifted, he did hear that, and he looked up. And he saw the door open, and got up and went to it. And there, just within the door, he came face to face with the thin figure of pain and woe.

To kill a fellow-creature is a frightful thing. At the time the act is committed, the murderer may have sound and convincing reasons (to him) for his act. But time and reflection may bring regret; even remorse; and this may live with him for many years. Examined in wakeful hours of the night or early morning, the reasons for the act may shed their cold logic, and may cease to be reasons and become mere excuses.

And these naked excuses may strip the murderer and show him to himself as he is. They may begin to hunt his soul, and to run into every little corner of his mind and every little nerve, in search of it. And if to kill a fellow-creature and to suffer the recurrent regret for an act of heated blood is a frightful thing, it is still more frightful to kill a fellow-creature and bury his body deep in an African jungle, and then, fifteen years later, at about midnight, to see the latch of your door lifted by the hand you had stilled and to see the man, looking much as he did fifteen years ago, walk into your home and claim your hospitality.

When the man in mackintosh and dungarees walked into the dining-rooms, Nameless stood still; stared; staggered against a table; supported himself by a hand, and said 'Oh!'

The other man said, 'Nameless!'

Then they looked at each other; Nameless with head thrust forward, mouth dropped; eyes wide; the visitor with a dull, glazed expression. If Nameless had not been the man he was—thick, bovine and costive—he would have flung up his arms and screamed. At that moment he felt the need of some such outlet, but did not know how to find it. The only dramatic expression he gave to the situation was to whisper instead of speak.

Twenty emotions came to life in his head and spine, and wrestled there. But they showed themselves only in his staring eyes and his whisper. His first thought, or rather, spasm, was 'Ghosts—Indigestion—Nervous—Breakdown.' His second, when he saw that the figure was substantial and real, was 'Impersonation'. But a slight movement on the part of the visitor dismissed that.

It was a little habitual movement which belonged only to that man; an unconscious twitching of the third finger of the left hand. He knew then that it was Gopak. Gopak, a little changed, but still, miraculously, thirty-two. Gopak, alive, breathing and real. No ghost. No phantom of the stomach. He was as certain of that as he was that fifteen years ago he had killed Gopak stone-dead and buried him.

The blackness of the moment was lightened by Gopak. In thin, flat tones he asked, 'May I sit down? I'm tired.' He sat down, and said: 'So tired. So tired.'

Nameless still held the table. He whispered: 'Gopak…

Gopak... But I—I *killed* you. I killed you in the jungle. You were dead. I know you were.'

Gopak passed his hand across his face. He seemed about to cry. 'I know you did. I know. That's all I can remember—about this earth. You killed me.' The voice became thinner and flatter. 'And I was so comfortable. So comfortable. It was—such a rest. Such a rest as you don't know. And then they came and—disturbed me. They woke me up. And brought me back.' He sat with shoulders sagged, arms drooping, hands hanging between knees. After the first recognition he did not look at Nameless; he looked at the floor.

'Came and disturbed you?' Nameless leaned forward and whispered the words. 'Woke you up? Who?'

'The Leopard Men.'

'The what?'

'The Leopard Men.' The watery voice said it as casually as if it were saying 'the night watchman'.

'The Leopard Men?' Nameless stared, and his fat face crinkled in an effort to take in the situation of a midnight visitation from a dead man, and the dead man talking nonsense. He felt his blood moving out of its course. He looked at his own hand to see if it was his own hand. He looked at the table to see if it was his table. The hand and the table were facts, and if the dead man was a fact—and he was—his story might be a fact. It seemed anyway as sensible as the dead man's presence. He gave a heavy sigh from the stomach.

'A-ah... The Leopard Men... Yes, I heard about them out there. Tales!'

Gopak slowly wagged his head. 'Not tales. They're real. If they weren't real—I wouldn't be here. Would I? I'd be at rest.'

Nameless had to admit this. He had heard many tales 'out there' about the Leopard Men, and had dismissed them as jungle yarns. But now, it seemed, jungle yarns had become commonplace fact in a little London shop.

The watery voice went on. 'They do it. I saw them. I came back in the middle of a circle of them. They killed a nigger to put his life into me. They wanted a white man—for their farm. So, they brought me back. You may not believe it. You wouldn't *want* to believe it. You wouldn't want to—see or know anything like them. And I wouldn't want any man to. But it's true. That's how I'm here.'

'But I left you absolutely dead. I made every test. It was three days before I buried you. And I buried you deep.'

'I know. But that wouldn't make any difference to them. It was a long time after when they came and brought me back. And I'm still dead, you know. It's only my body they brought back.' The voice trailed into a thread, 'And I'm so tired. So tired. I want to go back—to rest.'

Sitting in his prosperous eating-house, Nameless was in the presence of an achieved miracle, but the everyday, solid appointments of the eating-house wouldn't let him fully comprehend it. Foolishly, as he realized when he had spoken, he asked Gopak to explain what had happened. Asked a man who couldn't really be alive to explain how he came to be alive. It was like asking Nothing to explain Everything.

Constantly, as he talked, he felt his grasp on his own mind slipping. The surprise of a sudden visitor at a late hour; the shock of the arrival of a long-dead man; and the realization that this long-dead man was not a wraith, were too much for him.

During the next half-hour he found himself talking to Gopak as to the Gopak he had known seventeen years ago when they were partners. Then he would be halted by the freezing knowledge that he was talking to a dead man, and that a dead man was faintly answering him. He felt that the thing couldn't really have happened, but in the interchange of talk he kept forgetting the improbable side of it, and accepting it. With each recollection of the truth, his mind would clear and settle in one thought—'I've got to get rid of him. How am I going to get rid of him?'

'But how did you get here?'

'I escaped.' The words came slowly and thinly, and out of the body rather than the mouth.

'How.'

'I don't—know. I don't remember anything—except our quarrel. And being at rest.'

'But why come all the way here? Why didn't you stay on the coast?'

'I don't—know. But you're the only man I know. The only man I can remember.'

'But how did you find me?'

'I don't know. But I had to—find you. You're the only man—who can help me.'

'But how can I help you?'

The head turned weakly from side to side. 'I don't—know. But nobody else—can.'

Nameless stared through the window, looking on to the lamplit street and seeing nothing of it. The everyday being which had been his half an hour ago had been annihilated; the everyday beliefs and disbeliefs shattered and mixed together. But some shred of his old sense and his old standard remained. He must handle this situation. 'Well—what you want to do? What you going to do? I don't see how I can help you. And you can't stay here, obviously.' A demon of perversity sent a facetious notion into his head—introducing Gopak to his wife—'This is my dead friend.'

But on his last spoken remark Gopak made the effort of

raising his head and staring with the glazed eyes at Nameless. 'But I *must* stay here. There's nowhere else I can stay. I must stay here. That's why I came. You got to help me.'

'But you can't stay here. I got no room. All occupied. Nowhere for you to sleep.'

The wan voice said: 'That doesn't matter. I *don't* sleep.'

'Eh?'

'I *don't* sleep. I haven't slept since they brought me back. I can sit here—till you can think of some way of helping me.'

'But how *can* I?'

He again forgot the background of the situation, and began to get angry at the vision of a dead man sitting about the place waiting for him to think of something. 'How *can* I if you don't tell me how?'

'I don't—know. But you got to. *You* killed me. And I was dead—and comfortable. As it all came from you—killing me—you're responsible for me being—like this. So, you got to—help me. That's why I—came to you.'

'But what do you want me to do?'

'I don't—know. I can't—think. But nobody but you can help me. I had to come to you. Something brought me—straight to you. That means that you're the one—that can help me. Now I'm with you, something will—happen to help me. I feel it will. In time you'll—think of something.'

Nameless found his legs suddenly weak. He sat down and stared with a sick scowl at the hideous and the incomprehensible. Here was a dead man in his house—a man he had murdered in a moment of black temper—and he knew in his heart that he couldn't turn the man out. For one thing, he would have been afraid to touch him; he couldn't see himself touching him. For another, faced with the miracle of the presence of a fifteen-years-dead man, he doubted whether physical force or any material agency would be effectual in moving the man.

His soul shivered, as all men's souls shiver at the demonstration of forces outside their mental or spiritual horizon. He had murdered this man, and often, in fifteen years, he had repented the act. If the man's appalling story were true, then he had some sort of right to turn to Nameless. Nameless recognized that, and knew that whatever happened he couldn't turn him out. His hot-tempered sin had literally come home to him.

The wan voice broke into his nightmare. 'You go to rest Nameless. I'll sit here. You go to rest.' He put his face down to his hands and uttered a little moan. 'Oh, why can't I rest? Why can't I go back to my beautiful rest?'

Nameless came down early next morning with a half-hope that Gopak would not be there. But he was there, seated where Nameless had left him last night. Nameless made some tea, and showed him where he might wash. He washed listlessly, and crawled back to his seat, and listlessly drank the tea which Nameless brought to him.

To his wife and the kitchen helpers Nameless mentioned him as an old friend who had had a bit of a shock. 'Shipwrecked and knocked on the head. But quite harmless, and he won't be staying long. He's waiting for admission to a home. A good pal to me in the past, and it's the least I can do to let him stay here a few days. Suffers from sleeplessness and prefers to sit up at night. Quite harmless.'

But Gopak stayed more than a few days. He outstayed everybody. Even when the customers had gone, Gopak was still there.

On the first morning of his visit when the regular customers came in at mid-day, they looked at the odd, white figure sitting vacantly in the first pew, then stared, then moved away.

All avoided the pew in which he sat. Nameless explained him to them, but his explanation did not seem to relieve the slight tension which settled on the dining-room. The atmosphere was not so brisk and chatty as usual. Even those who had their backs to the stranger seemed to be affected by his presence.

At the end of the first day Nameless, noticing this, told him that he had arranged a nice corner of the front room upstairs, where he could sit by the window, and took his arm to take him upstairs. But Gopak feebly shook the hand away, and sat where he was. 'No. I don't want to go. I'll stay here. I'll stay here. I don't want to move.'

And he wouldn't move. After a few more pleadings Nameless realized with dismay that his refusal was definite; that it would be futile to press him or force him; that he was going to sit in that dining-room forever. He was as weak as a child and as firm as a rock.

He continued to sit in that first pew, and the customers continued to avoid it, and to give queer glances at it. It seemed that they half-recognized that he was something more than a fellow who had had a shock.

During the second week of his stay, three of the regular customers were missing, and more than one of those that remained made acidly facetious suggestions to Nameless that he park his lively friend somewhere else. He made things too exciting for them; all that whoopee took them off their work, and interfered with digestion. Nameless told them he would be staying only a day or so longer, but they found that this was untrue, and at the end of the second week eight of the regulars had found another place.

Each day, when the dinner-hour came, Nameless tried to get him to take a little walk, but he always refused.

He would go out only at night, and then never more than

two hundred yards from the shop. For the rest, he sat in his pew sometimes dozing in the afternoon, at other times staring at the floor. He took his food abstractedly, and never knew whether he had had food or not. He spoke only when questioned, and the burden of his talk was 'I'm so tired. So tired.'

One thing only seemed to arouse any light of interest in him—one thing only drew his eyes from the floor. That was the seventeen-year-old daughter of his host, who was known as Bubbles, and who helped with the waiting. And Bubbles seemed to be the only member of the shop and its customers, who did not shrink from him.

She knew nothing of the truth about him, but she seemed to understand him, and the only response he ever gave to anything was to her childish sympathy. She sat and chatted foolish chatter to him—'bringing him out of himself' she called it—and sometimes he would be brought out to the extent of a watery smile. He came to recognize her step, and would look up before she entered the room. Once or twice in the evening, when the shop was empty, and Nameless was sitting miserably with him, he would ask, without lifting his eyes. 'Where's Bubbles?' and would be told that Bubbles had gone to the pictures or was out at a dance, and would relapse into deeper vacancy. Nameless didn't like this. He was already visited by a curse which, in four weeks, had destroyed most of his business. Regular customers had dropped off two by two, and no new customers came to take their place. Strangers who dropped in once for a meal did not come again; they could not keep their eyes or their minds off the forbidding, white-faced figure sitting motionless in the first pew. At mid-day, when the place had been crowded and latecomers had to wait for a seat, it was now two-thirds empty; only a few of the most thick-skinned remained faithful.

And on top of this there was the interest of the dead

man in his daughter, an interest which seemed to be having an unpleasant effect. Nameless hadn't noticed it, but his wife had. 'Bubbles don't seem as bright and lively as she was. You noticed it lately? She's getting quiet—and a bit slack. Sits about a lot. Paler than she used to be.'

'Her age, perhaps.'

'No, she's not one of these thin, dark sort. No—it's something else. Just the last week or two I've noticed it. Off her food. Sits about doing nothing. No interest. May be nothing; just out of sorts, perhaps... How much longer's that horrible friend of yours going to stay?'

The horrible friend stayed some weeks longer—ten weeks in all—while Nameless watched his business drop to nothing and his daughter get pale and peevish. He knew the cause of it. There was no home in all England like his: no home that had a dead man sitting in it for ten weeks. A dead man brought, after a long time, from the grave, to sit and disturb his customers and take the vitality from his daughter. He couldn't tell this to anybody. Nobody would believe such nonsense.

But he *knew* that he was entertaining a dead man, and, knowing that a long-dead man was walking the earth, he could believe in any result of that fact. He could believe almost anything that he would have derided ten weeks ago. His customers had abandoned his shop, not because of the presence of a silent, white-faced man but because of the presence of a dead-living man.

Their minds might not know it, but their blood knew it. And as his business had been destroyed, so, he believed, would his daughter be destroyed. Her blood was not warming her; her blood told her only that this was a long-ago friend of her father's, and she was drawn to him.

It was at *this* point that Nameless, having no work to do,

began to drink. And it was well that he did so. For out of the drink came an idea, and with drat idea he freed himself from the curse upon him and his house.

The shop now served scarcely half a dozen customers at midday. It had become ill-kempt and dusty, and the service and the food were bad. Nameless took no trouble to be civil to his few customers. Often, when he was notably under drink, he went to the trouble of being very rude to them. They talked about this. They talked about the decline of his business and the dustiness of the shop and the bad food. They talked about his drinking, and, of course, exaggerated it.

And they talked about the queer fellow who sat there day after day and gave everybody the creeps. A few outsiders, hearing the gossip, came to the dining-rooms to see the queer fellow and the always-tight proprietor; but they did not come again, and there were not enough of the curious to keep the place busy. It went down until it served scarcely two customers a day. And Nameless went down with it into drink.

Then, one evening, out of the drink he fished an inspiration.

He took it downstairs to Gopak, who was sitting in his usual seat, hands hanging, eyes on the floor. 'Gopak—listen. You came here because I was the only man who could help you in your trouble. You listening?'

A faint 'Yes' was his answer.

'Well, now. You told me I'd got to think of something. I've thought of something... Listen. You say I'm responsible for your condition and got to get you out of it, because I killed you. I did. We had a row. *You* made me wild. You dared me. And what with that sun and the jungle and the insects, I wasn't meself I killed you. The moment it was done I could a-cut me right hand off. Because you and me were pals. I could a-cut me right hand off.

'I know. I felt that directly it was over. I knew you were suffering.'

'Ah!... I have suffered. And I'm suffering now.'

'Well, this is what I've thought. All your present trouble comes from me killing you in that jungle and burying you. An idea came to me. Do you think it would help you—do you think it would put you back to rest if I—if I—if I—killed you again?'

For some seconds Gopak continued to stare at the floor. Then his shoulders moved. Then, while Nameless watched every little response to his idea, the watery voice began. 'Yes. Yes. That's it. That's what I was waiting for. That's why I came here. I can see now. That's why I had to get here. Nobody else could kill me. Only you. I've got to be lolled again. Yes, I see. But nobody else—would be able—to kill me. Only the man who first killed me... Yes, you've found—what we're both—waiting for. Anybody else could shoot me—stab me—hang me—but they couldn't kill me. Only you. That's why I managed to get here and find you.'

The watery voice rose to a thin strength. 'That's it. And you must do it. Do it now. You don't want to, I know. But you must. You *must!*'

His head dropped and he stared at the floor. Nameless, too, stared at the floor. He was seeing things. He had murdered a man and had escaped all punishment save that of his own mind, which had been terrible enough. But now he was going to murder him again—not in a jungle but in a city; and he saw the slow points of the result.

He saw the arrest. He saw the first hearing. He saw the trial. He saw the cell. He saw the rope. He shuddered.

Then he saw the alternative—the breakdown of his life—a ruined business, poverty, the poorhouse, a daughter robbed of her health and perhaps dying, and always the curse of the dead-living man, who might follow him to the poorhouse. Better to end it all he thought. Rid himself of the curse which Gopak had brought upon him and his family, and then rid his family of himself with a revolver. Better to follow up his idea.

He got stiffly to his feet. The hour was late evening—half-past ten—and the streets were quiet. He had pulled down the shop-blinds and locked the door. The room was lit by one light at the further end.

He moved about uncertainly and looked at Gopak. 'Er—how would you—how shall I—'

Gopak said, 'You did it with a knife. Just under the heart. You must do it that way again.'

Nameless stood and looked at him for some seconds. Then, with an air of resolve, he shook himself. He walked quickly to the kitchen.

Three minutes later his wife and daughter heard a crash, as though a table had been overturned. They called but got no answer. When they came down they found him sitting in one of the pews, piping sweat from his forehead. He was white and shaking, and appeared to be recovering from a faint.

'Whatever's the matter? You all right?'

He waved them away. 'Yes, I'm all right. Touch of giddiness. Smoking too much, I think.'

'Mmmm. Or drinking—Where's your friend? Out for a walk?'

'No. He's gone off. Said he wouldn't impose any longer, and he'd go and find an infirmary.' He spoke weakly and found trouble in picking words. 'Didn't you hear that bang—when he shut the door?'

'I thought that was you fell down.'

'No. It was him when he went. I couldn't stop him.'

'Mmmm. Just as well, I think.' She looked about her. 'Things

THE DOCTOR'S GHOST

Dr Norman Macleod

A friend of mine, a medical man, once went on a fishing expedition with an old college acquaintance, an army surgeon, whom he had not met for many years, from his having been in India with his regiment. McDonald, the army surgeon, was a thorough Highlander, and slightly tinged with what is called the superstition of his countrymen, and at the time I speak of was liable to rather depressed spirits from an unsound liver. His native air was, however, rapidly renewing his youth; and when he and his old friend paced along the banks of the fishing stream in a lonely part of Argyllshire, and sent their lines like airy gossamers over the pools, and touched the water over a salmon's nose, so temptingly that the best-principled and wisest fish could not resist the bite, McDonald had apparently regained all his buoyancy of spirit.

They had been fishing together for about a week with great success, when McDonald proposed to pay a visit to a family with which he was acquainted, that would separate him from his friend for some days. But whenever he spoke of their intended separation, he sank down into his old gloomy state, at one time declaring that he felt as if they were never to meet again.

seem to a-gone wrong since he's been here.'

There was a general air of dustiness about the place. The tablecloths were dirty, not from use but from disuse. The windows were dim. A long knife, very dusty, was lying on the table under the window. In a corner by the door leading to the kitchen, unseen by her, lay a dusty mackintosh and dungaree, which appeared to have been tossed there. But it was over by the main door, near the first pew, that the dust was thickest—a long trail of it—greyish-white dust.

'Reely this place gets more and more slapdash. Why can't you attend to business? You didn't use to be like this. No wonder it's gone down, letting the place get into this state. Why don't you pull yourself together. Just *look* at that dust by the door. Looks as though somebody's been spilling ashes all over the place.'

Nameless looked at it, and his hands shook a little. But he answered, more firmly than before: 'Yes, I know. I'll have a proper clean-up tomorrow. I'll put it all to rights tomorrow. I been getting a bit slack.'

For the first time in ten weeks he smiled at them; a thin haggard smile, but a smile.

'I know. I felt that directly it was over. I knew you were suffering.'

'Ah!... I have suffered. And I'm suffering now.'

'Well, this is what I've thought. All your present trouble comes from me killing you in that jungle and burying you. An idea came to me. Do you think it would help you—do you think it would put you back to rest if I—if I—if I—killed you again?'

For some seconds Gopak continued to stare at the floor. Then his shoulders moved. Then, while Nameless watched every little response to his idea, the watery voice began. 'Yes. Yes. That's it. That's what I was waiting for. That's why I came here. I can see now. That's why I had to get here. Nobody else could kill me. Only you. I've got to be lolled again. Yes, I see. But nobody else—would be able—to kill me. Only the man who first killed me... Yes, you've found—what we're both—waiting for. Anybody else could shoot me—stab me—hang me—but they couldn't kill me. Only you. That's why I managed to get here and find you.'

The watery voice rose to a thin strength. 'That's it. And you must do it. Do it now. You don't want to, I know. But you must. You *must!*'

His head dropped and he stared at the floor. Nameless, too, stared at the floor. He was seeing things. He had murdered a man and had escaped all punishment save that of his own mind, which had been terrible enough. But now he was going to murder him again—not in a jungle but in a city; and he saw the slow points of the result.

He saw the arrest. He saw the first hearing. He saw the trial. He saw the cell. He saw the rope. He shuddered.

Then he saw the alternative—the breakdown of his life—a ruined business, poverty, the poorhouse, a daughter robbed of her health and perhaps dying, and always the curse of the dead-living man, who might follow him to the poorhouse. Better to end it all he thought. Rid himself of the curse which Gopak had brought upon him and his family, and then rid his family of himself with a revolver. Better to follow up his idea.

He got stiffly to his feet. The hour was late evening—half-past ten—and the streets were quiet. He had pulled down the shop-blinds and locked the door. The room was lit by one light at the further end.

He moved about uncertainly and looked at Gopak. 'Er—how would you—how shall I—'

Gopak said, 'You did it with a knife. Just under the heart. You must do it that way again.'

Nameless stood and looked at him for some seconds. Then, with an air of resolve, he shook himself. He walked quickly to the kitchen.

Three minutes later his wife and daughter heard a crash, as though a table had been overturned. They called but got no answer. When they came down they found him sitting in one of the pews, piping sweat from his forehead. He was white and shaking, and appeared to be recovering from a faint.

'Whatever's the matter? You all right?'

He waved them away. 'Yes, I'm all right. Touch of giddiness. Smoking too much, I think.'

'Mmmm. Or drinking—Where's your friend? Out for a walk?'

'No. He's gone off. Said he wouldn't impose any longer, and he'd go and find an infirmary.' He spoke weakly and found trouble in picking words. 'Didn't you hear that bang—when he shut the door?'

'I thought that was you fell down.'

'No. It was him when he went. I couldn't stop him.'

'Mmmm. Just as well, I think.' She looked about her. 'Things

My friend tried to rally him, but in vain. They parted at the trouting stream, McDonald's route being across a mountain pass, with which, however, he had been well-acquainted in his youth, though the road was lonely and wild in the extreme.

The doctor returned early in the evening to his resting-place, which was a shepherd's house lying on the very outskirts of the 'settlements', and beside a foaming mountain stream. The shepherd's only attendants at the time were two herd lads and three dogs. Attached to the hut, and communicating with it by a short passage, was rather a comfortable room which 'the Laird' had fitted up to serve as a sort of lodge for himself in the midst of his shooting-ground, and which he had put for a fortnight at the disposal of my friend.

Shortly after sunset, on the day I mention, the wind began to rise suddenly to a gale, the rain descended in torrents, and the night became extremely dark. The shepherd seemed uneasy, and several times went to the door to inspect the weather. At last he roused the fears of the doctor for McDonald's safety, by expressing the *hope* that by this time he was 'owre that awfu' black moss, and across the red burn.'

Every traveller in the Highlands knows how rapidly these mountain streams rise, and how confusing the moor becomes in a dark night. The confusion of memory once a doubt is suggested, the utter mystery of places, becomes, as I know from experience, quite indescribable.

'The black moss and red burn' were words that were never after forgot by the doctor, from the strange feelings they produced when first heard that night; for there came into his mind terrible thoughts and forebodings about poor McDonald, and reproaches for never having considered his possible danger in attempting such a journey alone. In vain the shepherd assured him that he must have reached a place of safety before the darkness and the storm came on. A presentiment which he could not cast off made him so miserable that he could hardly refrain from tears. But nothing could be done to relieve the anxiety now become so painful.

The doctor at last retired to bed about midnight. For a long time he could not sleep. The raging of the stream below the small window, and the *thuds* of the storm, made him feverish and restless. But at last he fell into a sound and dreamless sleep. Out of this, however, he was suddenly roused by a peculiar noise in his room, not very loud, but utterly indescribable. He heard tap, tap, tap at the window, and he knew, from the relation which the wall of the room bore to the rock, that the glass could not be touched by human hand.

After listening for a moment, and forcing himself to smile at his nervousness, he turned round, and began again to seek repose. But now a noise began too near and loud to make sleep possible. Starting and sitting up in bed, he heard repeated in rapid succession, as if someone was spitting in anger, and close to his bed,—'Fit! fit! fit!' and then a prolonged 'whir-r-r' from another part of the room, while every chair began to move, and the table to jerk!

The doctor remained in breathless silence, with every faculty intensely acute. He frankly confessed that he heard his heart beating, for the sound was so unearthly, so horrible, and something seemed to come so near him, that he began seriously to consider whether or not he had some attack of fever which affected his brain—for, remember, he had not tasted a drop of the shepherd's small store of whisky! He felt his pulse, composed his spirits, and compelled himself to exercise a calm judgement. Straining his eyes to discover anything, he plainly saw at last a white object moving, but without sound, before him. He knew that the door was shut and the window also.

An overpowering conviction then seized him, which he could not resist, that his friend McDonald was dead! By an effort he seized a lucifer-box on a chair beside him, and struck a light. No white object could be seen. The room appeared to be as when he went to bed. The door was shut. He looked at his watch, and particularly marked that the hour was twenty-two minutes past three. But the match was hardly extinguished when, louder than ever, the same unearthly cry of 'Fit! fit! fit!' was heard, followed by the same horrible 'whir-rrr-r', which made his teeth chatter. Then the movement of the table and every chair in the room was resumed with increased violence, while the tapping on the window was heard above the storm. There was no bell in the room, but the doctor, on hearing all this frightful confusion of sounds again repeated, and beholding the white object moving towards him in terrible silence, began to thump the wooden partition and to shout at the top of his voice for the shepherd, and having done so, he dived his head under the blankets!

The shepherd soon made his appearance, in his night-shirt, with a small oil-lamp, or 'crusey', over his head, anxiously inquiring as he entered the room:

'What is't, doctor? What's wrong? Pity me, are ye ill?'

'Very!' cried the doctor. But before he could give any explanation a loud whir-r-r was heard, with the old cry of 'Fit!' close to the shepherd, while two chairs fell at his feet! The shepherd sprang back, with a half scream of terror the lamp was dashed to the ground, and the door violently shut.

'Come back!' shouted the doctor. 'Come back, Duncan, instantly, I command you!'

The shepherd opened the door very partially, and said, in terrified accents:

'Gude be aboot us, that was awfu'! What under heaven is't?'

'Heaven knows, Duncan,' ejaculated the doctor with agitated voice, 'but do pick up the lamp, and I shall strike a light.'

Duncan did so in no small fear; but as he made his way to the bed in the darkness to get a match from the doctor, something caught his foot; he fell; and then, amidst the same noises and tumults of chairs, which immediately filled the apartment, the 'Fit! fit! fit! fit!' was prolonged with more vehemence than ever!

The doctor sprang up, and made his way out of the room, but his feet were several times tripped by some unknown power, so that he had the greatest difficulty in reaching the door without a fall. He was followed by Duncan, and both rushed out of the room, shutting the door after them. A new light having been obtained, they both returned with extreme caution, and, it must be added, real fear, in the hope of finding some cause or other for all those terrifying signs.

Would it surprise our readers to hear that they searched the room in vain—that, after minutely examining under the table, chairs, bed, everywhere, and with the door shut, not a trace could be found of anything? Would they believe that they heard during the day how poor McDonald had staggered, half dead from fatigue, into his friend's house, and falling into a fit, had died at *twenty-two minutes past three* that morning? We do not ask anyone to accept all of this as true. But we pledge our honour to the following facts:

The doctor, after the day's fishing was over, had packed his rod so as to take it into his bedroom; but he had left a minnow attached to the hook. A white cat left in the room swallowed the minnow and was hooked. The unfortunate gourmand had vehemently protested against this intrusion into its upper lip by the violent 'Fit! fit! fit!' with which she tried to spit the hook out; the reel added the mysterious 'whir-r-r-r'; and the disengaged line, getting entangled in the legs of the chairs and table, as the hooked cat attempted to flee from her tormentor, set the furniture in motion, and tripped up both shepherd and doctor; while an ivy branch kept tapping at the window! Will anyone doubt the existence of ghosts and a spirit-world after this?

I have only to add that the doctor's skill was employed during the night in cutting the hook out of the cat's lip, while his poor patient, yet most impatient, was held by the shepherd in a bag, the head alone of the puss, with hook and minnow, being visible. McDonald made his appearance in a day or two, rejoicing once more to see his friend, and greatly enjoying the ghost story.

THE PHANTOM 'RICKSHAW

Rudyard Kipling

May no ill dreams disturb my rest,
Nor Powers of Darkness me molest.

                            Evening Hymn

One of the few advantages that India has over England is a great knowability. After five years' service a man is directly or indirectly acquainted with the two or three hundred civilians in his province, all the messes of ten or twelve regiments and batteries, and some fifteen hundred other people of the non-official caste. In ten years his knowledge should be doubled, and at the end of twenty he knows, or knows something about, every Englishman in the Empire, and may travel anywhere and everywhere without paying hotel-bills.

Globe-trotters who expect entertainment as a right have, even within my memory, blunted this open-heartedness, but nonetheless today, if you belong to the Inner Circle and are neither a Bear nor a Black Sheep, all houses are open to you, and our small world is very, very kind and helpful.

Rickett of Kamartha stayed with Polder of Kumaon some fifteen years ago. He meant to stay two nights, but was knocked down by rheumatic fever, and for six weeks disorganized Polder's establishment, stopped Polder's work, and nearly died in Polder's bedroom. Polder behaves as though he had been placed under eternal obligation by Rickett, and yearly sends the little Ricketts a box of presents and toys. It is the same everywhere. The men who do not take the trouble to conceal from you their opinion that you are an incompetent ass, and the women who blacken your character and misunderstand your wife's amusements, will work themselves to the bone in your behalf if you fall sick or into serious trouble.

Heatherlegh, the doctor, kept, in addition to his regular practice, a hospital on his private account—an arrangement of loose boxes for incurables, his friend called it—but it was really a sort of fitting-up shed for craft that had been damaged by the stress of weather. The weather in India is often sultry, and since the tale of bricks is always a fixed quantity, and the only liberty allowed is permission to work overtime and get no thanks, men occasionally break down and become as mixed as the metaphors in this sentence.

Heatherlegh is the dearest doctor that ever was, and his invariable prescription to all his patients is, 'Lie low, go slow, and keep cool.' He says that more men are killed by overwork than the importance of this world justifies. He maintains that overwork slew Pansay, who died under his hands about three years ago. He has, of course, the right to speak authoritatively, and he laughs at my theory that there was a crack in Pansay's head and a little bit of the Dark World came through and pressed him to death. 'Pansay went off the handle,' says Heatherlegh, 'after the stimulus of long leave at Home. He may or he may not have behaved like a blackguard to Mrs Keith-Wessington. My notion is that the work of the Katabundi Settlement ran him off his legs, and that he took to brooding and making much of an ordinary E & O. flirtation. He certainly was engaged to Miss Mannering, and she certainly broke off the engagement. Then he took a feverish chill and all that nonsense about ghosts developed. Overwork started his illness, kept it alight, and killed him, poor devil. Write him off to the system that uses one man to do the work of two and a half men.'

I do not believe this. I use to sit up with Pansay sometimes when Heatherlegh was called out to patients and I happened to be within claim. The man would make me most unhappy by describing in a low, even voice, the procession that was always passing at the bottom of the bed. He had a sick man's command of language. When he recovered I suggested that he should write out the whole affair from beginning to end, knowing that ink might assist him to ease his mind.

He was in a high fever while he was writing, and the blood-and-thunder magazine diction he adopted did not calm him. Two months afterwards he was reported fit for duty, but, in spite of the fact that he was urgently needed to help an undermanned Commission stagger through a deficit, he preferred to die; vowing at the last that he was hag-ridden. I got his manuscript before he died, and this is his version of the affair, dated 1885, exactly as he wrote it:

My doctor tells me that I need rest and change of air. It is not improbable that I shall get both ere long—rest that neither the red-coated messenger nor the mid-day gun can break, and change of air far beyond that which any homeward-bound steamer can give me. In the meantime I am resolved to stay where I am; and, in flat defiance of my doctor's orders, to take all the world into my confidence. You shall learn for yourselves the precise nature of my malady, and shall, too, judge for yourselves whether any man born of woman on this weary earth was ever so tormented as I.

Speaking now as a condemned criminal might speak ere the drop-bolts are drawn, my story, wild and hideously improbable as it may appear, demands at least attention. That it will ever receive credence I utterly disbelieve. Two months ago I should have scouted as mad or drunk the man who had dared tell me the like. Two months ago I was the happiest man in India. Today, from Peshawar to the sea there is no one more wretched. My doctor and I are the only two who know this. His explanation is, that my brain, digestion and eyesight are all slightly affected; giving rise to my frequent and persistent 'delusions'. Delusions, indeed I call him a fool; but he attends me still with the same unwearied smile, the same bland professional manner, the same neatly-trimmed red whiskers, till I begin to suspect that I am an ungrateful, evil-tempered invalid. But you shall judge for yourselves.

Three years ago it was my fortune—my great misfortune—to sail from Gravesend to Bombay, on return from a long leave, with one Agnes Keith-Wessington, wife of an officer on the Bombay side. It does not in the least concern you to know what manner of woman she was. Be content with the knowledge that, ere the voyage had ended, both she and I were desperately and unreasoningly in love with one another. Heaven knows that I can make the admission now without one particle of vanity. In matters of this sort there is always one who gives and another who accepts. From the first day of our ill-omened attachment, I was conscious that Agnes's passion was a stronger, a more dominant, and—if I may use the expression—a purer sentiment than mine. Whether she recognized the fact then, I do not know. Afterwards it was bitterly plain to both of us.

Arrived at Bombay in the spring of the year, we went our respective ways, to meet no more for the next three or four months, when my leave and her love took us both to Simla.

There we spent the season together; and there my fire *of* straw burnt itself out to a pitiful end with the closing year. I attempt no excuse. I make no apology. Mrs Wessington had given up much for my sake, and was prepared to give up all. From my own lips, in August 1882, she learnt that I was sick of her presence, tired of her company, and weary of the sound of her voice. Ninety-nine women out of a hundred would have wearied of me as I wearied of them; seventy-five of that number would have promptly avenged themselves by active and obtrusive flirtation with other men. Mrs Wessington was the hundredth. On her neither my openly-expressed aversion nor the cutting brutalities with which I garnished our interviews had the least effect.

'Jack, darling!' was her one eternal cuckoo cry: 'I'm sure it's all a mistake—a hideous mistake; and we'll be good friends again some day. *Please* forgive me, Jack, dear.'

I was the offender, and I knew it. That knowledge transformed my pity into passive endurance, and, eventually, into blind hate—the same instinct, I suppose, which prompts a man to savagely stamp on the spider he has but half-killed. And with this hate in my bosom the season of 1882 came to an end.

Next year we met again at Simla—she with her monotonous face and timid attempts at reconciliation, and I with loathing of her in every fibre of my frame. Several times I could not avoid meeting her alone; and on each occasion her words were identically the same. Still the unreasoning wail that it was all a 'mistake'; and still the hope of eventually 'making friends'. I might have seen, had I cared to look, that that hope only was keeping her alive. She grew more wan and thin month by month. You will agree with me, at least, that such conduct would have driven any one to despair. It was uncalled for; childish; unwomanly. I maintain that she was much to blame. And again, sometimes, in the black, fever-stricken night-watches,

I have begun to think that I might have been a little kinder to her. But that really *is* a 'delusion'. I could not have continued pretending to love her when I didn't; could I? It would have been unfair to us both.

Last year we met again—on the same terms as before. The same weary appeals, and the same curt answers from my lips. At least I would make her see how wholly wrong and hopeless were her attempts at resuming the old relationship. As the season wore on, we fell apart—that is to say, she found it difficult to meet me, for I had other and more absorbing interests to attend to. When I think it over quietly in my sickroom, the season of 1884 seems a confused nightmare wherein light and shade were fantastically intermingled—my courtship of little Kitty Mannering; my hopes, doubts, and fears; our long rides together; my trembling avowal of attachment; her reply; and now and again a vision of a white face flitting by in the 'rickshaw with the black and white liveries I once watched for so earnestly; the wave of Mrs Wessington's gloved hand; and, when she met me alone, which was but seldom, the irksome monotony of her appeal. I loved Kitty Mannering; honestly, heartily loved her, and with my love for her grew my hatred for Agnes. In August, Kitty and I were engaged. The next day I met those accursed 'magpie' jhampanies at the back of Jakko, and, moved by some passing sentiment of pity, stopped to tell Mrs Wessington everything. She knew it already.

'So I hear you're engaged, Jack dear.' Then, without a moment's pause: 'I'm sure it's all a mistake—a hideous mistake. We shall be as good friends some day, Jack, as we ever were.'

My answer might have made even a man wince. It cut the dying woman before me like the blow of a whip. 'Please forgive me, Jack; I didn't mean to make you angry; but it's true, it's true!'

And Mrs Wessington broke down completely. I turned away and left her to finish her journey in peace, feeling, but only for a moment or two, that I had been an unutterably mean hound. I looked back, and saw that she had turned her 'rickshaw with the idea, I suppose, of overtaking me.

The scene and its surroundings were photographed on my memory. The rain-swept sky (we were at the end of the wet weather), the sodden, dingy pines, the muddy road, and the black powder-riven cliffs formed a gloomy background against which the black and white liveries of the jhampanies, the yellow-panelled 'rickshaw and Mrs Wessington's down-bowed golden head stood out clearly. She was holding her handkerchief in her left hand and was leaning back exhausted against the 'rickshaw cushions. I turned my horse up a bypath near the Sanjowlie Reservoir and literally ran away. Once I fancied I heard a faint call of 'Jack!'. This may have been imagination. I never stopped to verify it. Ten minutes later I came across Kitty on horseback; and, in the delight of a long ride with her, forgot all about the interview.

A week later Mrs Wessington died, and the inexpressible burden of her existence was removed from my life. I went Plainsward perfectly happy. Before three months were over I had forgotten all about her, except that at times the discovery of some of her old letters reminded me unpleasantly of our bygone relationship. By January I had disinterred what was left of our correspondence from among my scattered belongings and had burnt it. At the beginning of April of this year, 1885, I was at Simla—semi-deserted Simla—once more, and was deep in lover's talks and walks with Kitty. It was decided that we should be married at the end of June. You will understand, therefore, that, loving Kitty as I did, I am not saying too much when I pronounce myself to have been, at that time, the happiest man in India.

Fourteen delightful days passed almost before I noticed their flight. Then, aroused to the sense of what was proper among mortals, circumstanced as we were, I pointed out to Kitty that an engagement ring was the outward and visible sign of her dignity as an engaged girl; and that she must forthwith come to Hamilton's to be measured for one. Up to that moment, I give you my word, we had completely forgotten so trivial a matter. To Hamilton's we accordingly went on the 15th of April 1885. Remember that—whatever my doctor may say to the contrary—I was then in perfect health, enjoying a well-balanced mind and an *absolutely* tranquil spirit. Kitty and I entered Hamilton's shop together, and there, regardless of the order of affairs, I measured Kitty for the ring in the presence of the amused assistant. The ring was a sapphire with two diamonds. We men rode out down the slope that leads to the Combermere Bridge and Peliti's shop.

While my Waler was cautiously feeling his way over the loose shale, and Kitty was laughing and chattering at my side-while all Simla, that is to say as much of it as had then come from the plains, was grouped round the reading-room and Peliti's verandah, I was aware that someone, apparently at a vast distance, was calling me by my Christian name. It struck me that I had heard the voice before, but when and where I could not at once determine. In the short space it took to cover the road between the path from Hamilton's shop and the first plank of the Combermere Bridge I had thought over half a dozen people who might have committed such a solecism, and had eventually decided that it must have been some singing in my ears. Immediately opposite Peliti's shop my eye was arrested by the sight of four jhampanies in 'magpie' livery, pulling a yellow-panelled, cheap, bazar 'rickshaw. In a moment my mind flew back to the previous season and Mrs Wessington, with a sense of irritation and disgust. Was it not enough that the woman was dead and done with, without her black and white servitors reappearing to spoil the day's happiness? Whoever employed them now, I thought I would call upon, and ask as a personal favour to change her jhampanies' livery. I would hire the men myself, and, if necessary, buy their coats from off their backs. It is impossible to say here what a flood of undesirable memories their presence evoked.

'Kitty,' I cried, 'there are poor Mrs Wessington's jhampanies turned up again! I wonder who has them now?'

Kitty had known Mrs Wessington slightly last season, and had always been interested in the sickly woman.

'What? Where?' she asked. 'I can't see them anywhere.'

Even as she spoke, her horse, swerving from a laden mule, threw himself directly in front of the advancing 'rickshaw. I had scarcely time to utter a word of warning when, to my unutterable horror, horse and rider passed *through* men and carriage as if they had been thin air.

'What's the matter?' cried Kitty; 'what made you call out so foolishly, Jack? If I *am* engaged I don't want all creation to know about it. There was lots of space between the mule and the verandah; and, if you think I can't ride—There!'

Whereupon the wilful Kitty set off, her dainty little head in the air, at a hand-gallop in the direction of the Bandstand; fully expecting, as she herself afterwards told me, that I should follow her. What was the matter? Nothing indeed. Either that I was mad or drunk, or that Simla was haunted with devils. I reined in my impatient cob, and turned round. The 'rickshaw had turned too, and now stood immediately facing me, near the left railing of the Combermere Bridge.

'Jack! Jack, darling!' (There was no mistake about the words this time: they rang through my brain as if they had been shouted in my ear.) 'It's some hideous mistake, I'm sure. *Please* forgive me, Jack, and lets' be friends again.'

The 'rickshaw-hood had fallen back, and inside, as I hope and pray daily for the death I dread by night, sat Mrs Keith-

Wessington, handkerchief in hand, and golden head bowed on her breast.

How long I stared motionless I do not know. Finally, I was aroused by my syce taking the Waler's bridle and asking whether I was ill. From the horrible to the commonplace is but a step. I tumbled off my horse and dashed, half-fainting, into Peliti's for a glass of cherry-brandy. There two or three couples were gathered round the coffee-tables discussing the gossip of the day. Their trivialities were more comforting to me just then than the consolations of religion could have been. I plunged into the midst of the conversation at once; chatted, laughed and jested with a face (when I caught a glimpse of it in a mirror) as white and drawn as that of a corpse. Three or four men noticed my condition; and, evidently setting it down to the results of over-many pegs, charitably endeavoured to draw me apart from the rest of the loungers. But I refused to be led away. I wanted the company of my kind—as a child rushes into the midst of the dinner-party after a fright in the dark. I must have talked for about ten minutes or so, though it seemed an eternity to me, when I heard Kitty's clear voice outside enquiring for me. In another minute she had entered the shop, prepared to upbraid me for failing so signally in my duties. Something in my face stopped her.

'Why, Jack,' she cried, 'what *have* you been doing? What *has* happened? Are you ill?' Thus driven into a direct lie, I said that the sun had been a little too much for me. it was close upon five o'clock of a cloudy April afternoon, and the sun had been hidden all day. I saw my mistake as soon as the words were out of my mouth: attempted to recover it; blundered hopelessly and followed Kitty, in a regal rage, out of doors, amid the smiles of my acquaintances. I made some excuse (I have forgotten what) on the score of my feeling faint; and cantered away to my hotel, leaving Kitty to finish the ride by herself.

In my room I sat down and tried calmly to reason out the matter. Here was I, Theobald Jack Pansay, a well-educated Bengal Civilian in the year of grace, 1885, presumably sane, certainly healthy, driven in terror from my sweetheart's side by the apparition of a woman who had been dead and buried eight months ago. These were facts that I could not blink. Nothing was further from my thought than any memory of Mrs Wessington when Kitty and I left Hamilton's shop. Nothing was more utterly commonplace than the stretch of wall opposite Peliti's. It was broad daylight. The road was full of people; and yet here, look you, in defiance of every law of probability, in direct outrage of Nature's ordinance, there had appeared to me a face from the grave.

Kitty's Arab had gone *through* the 'rickshaw: so that my first hope that some woman marvellously like Mrs Wessington had hired the carriage and the coolies with their old livery was lost. Again and again I went round this treadmill of thought; and again and again gave up baffled and in despair. The voice was as inexplicable as the apparition. I had originally some wild notion of confiding it all to Kitty; of begging her to marry me at once; and in her arms defying the ghostly occupant of the 'rickshaw. 'After all,' I argued, 'the presence of the 'rickshaw is in itself enough to prove the existence of a spectral illusion. One may see ghosts of men and women, but surely never coolies and carriages. The whole thing is absurd. Fancy the ghost of a hillman!'

Next morning I sent a penitent note to Kitty, imploring her to overlook my strange conduct of the previous afternoon. My Divinity was still very wroth, and a personal apology was necessary. I explained, with a fluency born of night-long pondering over a falsehood, that I had been attacked with a sudden palpitation of the heart—the result of indigestion. This eminently practical solution had its effect: and Kitty and I rode out that afternoon with the shadow of my first lie dividing us.

Nothing would please her save a canter round Jakko. With my nerves still unstrung from the previous night I feebly protested against the notion, suggesting Observatory Hill, Jutogh, the Boileaugunge road—anything rather than the Jakko round. Kitty was angry and a little hurt; so I yielded from fear of provoking further misunderstanding, and we set out together towards Chhota Simla. We walked a greater part of the way, and, according to our custom, cantered from a mile or so below the Convent to the stretch of level road by the Sanjowlie Reservoir. The wretched horses appeared to fly, and my heart beat quicker and quicker as we neared the crest of the ascent. My mind had been full of Mrs Wessington all afternoon; and every inch of the Jakko road bore witness to our old-time walks and talks. The bowlders were full of it; the pines sang it aloud overhead; the rain-fed torrents giggled and chuckled unseen over the shameful story; and the wind in my ears chanted the iniquity aloud.

As a fitting climax, in the middle of the level men call the Ladies' Mile the horror was awaiting me. No other 'rickshaw was in sight—only the four black and white jhampanies, the yellow-panelled carriage, and the golden head of the woman within—all apparently just as I had left them eight months and one fortnight ago! For an instant I fancied that Kitty *must* see what I saw—we were so marvellously sympathetic in all things.

Her next words undeceived me—'Not a soul in sight! Come along, Jack, and I'll race you to the Reservoir buildings!' Her wiry little Arab was off like a bird, my Waler following close behind, and in this order we dashed under the cliffs. Half a minute brought us within fifty yards of the 'rickshaw. I pulled my Waler and fell back a little. The 'rickshaw was directly in the middle of the road; and once more the Arab passed through it, my horse following. 'Jack! Jack dear! *Please* forgive me,' rang with a wail in my ears, and, after an interval: 'It's all a mistake, a hideous mistake!'

I spurred my horse like a man possessed. When I turned my head at the Reservoir works, the black and white liveries were still waiting—patiently waiting—under the gray hillside, and the wind brought me a mocking echo of the words I had just heard. Kitty bantered me a good deal on my silence throughout the remainder of the ride. I had been talking up till then wildly and at random. To save my life I could not speak afterwards, naturally, and from Sanjowlie to the Church wisely held my tongue.

I was to dine with the Mannerings that night, and had barely time to canter home to dress. On the road to Elysium Hill I overheard two men talking together in the dusk—'It's a curious thing,' said one, 'how completely all trace of it disappeared. You know my wife was insanely fond of the woman (never could see anything in her myself), and wanted me to pick up her old 'rickshaw and coolies if they were to be got for love or money. Morbid sort of fancy I call it; but I've got to do what the Memsahib tells me. Would you believe that the man she hired it from tells me that all four of the men—they were brothers—died of cholera on the way to Haridwar, poor devils; and the 'rickshaw has been broken up by the man himself. Told me he never used a dead Memsahib's 'rickshaw. Spoilt his luck. Queer notion, wasn't it? Fancy poor little Mrs Wessington spoiling any one's luck except her own!' I laughed aloud at this point; and my laugh jarred on me as I uttered it. So there *were* ghosts of 'rickshaws after all, and ghostly employments in the other world! How much did Mrs Wessington give her men? What were their hours? Where did they go?

And for visible answer to my last question I saw the infernal Thing blocking my path in the twilight. The dead travel fast, and by short cuts unknown to ordinary coolies. I laughed aloud a second time and checked my laughter suddenly, for I was afraid I was going mad. Mad to a certain extent I must have been, for I recollect that I reined in my horse at the head of the 'rickshaw, and politely wished Mrs Wessington 'Good-evening'. Her answer was one I knew only too well. I listened to the end; and replied that I had heard it all before, but should be delighted if she had anything further to say; some malignant devil stronger than I must have entered into me that evening, for I have a dim recollection of talking the commonplaces of the day for five minutes to the Thing in front of me.

'Mad as a hatter, poor devil—or drunk. Max, try and get him to come home.'

Surely *that* was not Mrs Wessington's voice! The two men had overheard me speaking to the empty air, and had returned to look after me. They were very kind and considerate, and from their words evidently gathered that I was extremely drunk. I thanked them confusedly and cantered away to my hotel, there changed, and arrived at the Mannerings' ten minutes late. I pleaded the darkness of the night as an excuse; was rebuked by Kitty for my unlover-like tardiness; and sat down.

The conversation had already become general; and under cover of it, I was addressing some tender small talk to my sweetheart when I was aware that at the further end of the table a short red-whiskered man was describing, with much broidery, his encounter with a mad unknown that evening.

A few sentences convinced me that he was repeating the incident of half an hour ago. In the middle of the story he looked around for applause, as professional story tellers do, caught my eye, and straightway collapsed. There was a moment's awkward silence, and the red-whiskered man muttered something to the effect that he had 'forgotten the rest', thereby sacrificing a reputation as a good storyteller which he had built up for six seasons past. I blessed him from the bottom of my heart, and—went on with my fish.

In the fullness of time that dinner came to an end; and with genuine regret I tore myself away from Kitty—as certain as I was of my own existence that it would be waiting for me outside the door. The red-whiskered man, who had been introduced to me as Dr Heatherlegh of Simla, volunteered to bear me company as far as our roads lay together. I accepted his offer with gratitude.

My instinct had not deceived me. It lay in readiness in the Mall, and, in what seemed devilish mockery of our ways, with a lighted head lamp. The red-whiskered man went to the point at once, in a manner that showed he had been thinking over it all dinner-time.

'I say, Pansay, what the deuce was the matter with you this evening on the Elysium Road?' The suddenness of the question wrenched an answer from me before I was aware.

'That!' said I, pointing to it.

'*That* may be either D.T. or Eyes for aught I know. Now you don't liquor. I saw as much at dinner, so it can't be D.T. There's nothing whatever where you're pointing, though you're sweating and trembling with fright, like a scared pony. Therefore, I conclude that it's Eyes. And I ought to understand all about them. Come along home with me. I'm on the Blessington lower road.'

To my intense delight the 'rickshaw instead of waiting for us kept about twenty yards ahead—and this, too, whether we walked, trotted, or cantered. In the course of that long night ride I had told my companion almost as much as I have told you here.

'Well, you've spoilt one of the best tales I've ever laid tongue to,' said he, 'but I'll forgive you for the sake of what you've gone through. Now come home and do what I tell you; and when I've cured you, young man, let this be a lesson to you to steer clear of women and indigestible food till the day of your death.'

The 'rickshaw kept steady in front; and my red-whiskered friend seemed to derive great pleasure from my account of its exact whereabouts.

'Eyes, Pansay—all Eyes, Brain and Stomach. And the greatest of these three is Stomach. You've too much conceited Brain, too little Stomach, and thoroughly unhealthy Eyes. Get your Stomach straight and the rest follows. And all that's French for a liver pill. I'll take sole medical charge of you from this hour! For you're too interesting a phenomenon to be passed over.'

By this time we were deep in the shadow of the Blessington lower road and the 'rickshaw came to a dead stop under a pine-clad, overhanging shale cliff. Instinctively I halted too, giving my reason, Heatherlegh rapped out an oath.

'Now, if you think I'm going to spend a cold night on the hillside for the sake of a Stomach-cum-Brain-cum-Eye illusion——Lord, ha' mercy! What's that?'

There was a muffled report, a blinding smother of dust just in front of us, a crack, the noise of rent boughs, and about ten yards of the cliff-side—pines, undergrowth, and all—slid down into the road below, completely blocking it up. The uprooted trees swayed and tottered for a moment like drunken giants in the gloom, and then fell prone among their fellows with a thunderous crash. Our two horses stood motionless and sweating with fear. As soon as the rattle of falling earth and stone had subsided, my companion muttered: 'Man, if we'd gone forward we should have been ten feet deep in our graves by now. "There are more things in heaven and earth"... Come home, Pansay, and thank God. I want a peg badly.'

We retraced our way over the Church Ridge, and I arrived at Dr Heatherlegh's house shortly after midnight.

His attempts towards my cure commenced almost immediately, and for a week I never left his sight. Many a time in the course of that week did I bless the good fortune which had thrown me in contact with Simla's best and kindest doctor. Day by day my spirits grew lighter and more equable. Day by day, too, I became more and more inclined to fall in with Heatherlegh's 'spectral illusion' theory, implicating the eyes, brain, and stomach. I wrote to Kitty, telling her that a slight sprain caused by a fall from my horse kept me indoors for a few days; and that I should be recovered before she had time to regret my absence.

Heatherlegh's treatment was simple to a degree. It consisted of liver pills, cold-water baths, and strong exercise, taken in the dusk or at early dawn—for, as he sagely observed: 'A man with a sprained ankle doesn't walk a dozen miles a day, and your young woman might be wondering if she saw you.'

At the end of the week, after much examination of pupil and pulse, and strict injunctions as to diet and pedestrianism, Heatherlegh dismissed me as brusquely as he had taken charge of me. Here is his parting benediction: 'Man, I certify to your mental cure, and that's as much as to say I've cured most of your bodily ailments. Now, get your traps out of this as soon as you can; and be off to make love to Miss Kitty.'

I was endeavouring to express my thanks for his kindness. He cut me short.

'Don't think I did this because I like you. I gather that you've behaved like a blackguard all through. But, all the same, you're a phenomenon, and as queer a phenomenon as you are a blackguard. No!'—checking me a second time—'not a rupee, please. Go out and see if you can find the eyes-brain-and-stomach business again. I'll give you a lakh for each time you see it.'

Half an hour later I was in the Mannerings' drawing-room with Kitty—drunk with the intoxication of the present happiness and the foreknowledge that I should never more be troubled with its hideous presence. Strong in the sense of my new-found security, I proposed a ride at once; and, by preference, a canter round Jakko.

Never had I felt so well, so overladen with vitality and mere animal spirits, as I did on the afternoon of the 30th of April. Kitty was delighted at the change in my appearance, and complimented me on it in her delightfully frank and outspoken manner. We left the Mannerings' house together, laughing and talking, and cantered along the Chhota Simla road as of old.

I was in haste to reach the Sanjowlie Reservoir and there make my assurance doubly sure. The horses did their best, but seemed all too slow to my impatient mind. Kitty was astonished at my boisterousness. 'Why, Jack!' she cried at last, 'you are behaving like a child. What are you doing?'

We were just below the Convent, and from sheer wantonness I was making my Waler plunge and curvet across the road as I tickled it with the loop of my riding-whip.

'Doing?' I answered; 'nothing, dear. That's just it. If you'd been doing nothing for a week except lie up, you'd be as riotous as I.

'Singing and murmuring in your feastful mirth,
    Joying to feel yourself alive;
Lord over Nature, Lord of the visible Earth,
    Lord of the senses five.'

My quotation was hardly out of my lips before we had rounded the corner above the Convent; and a few yards further on could see across to Sanjowlie. In the centre of the level road stood the black and white liveries, the yellow-panelled 'rickshaw, and Mrs Keith-Wessington. I pulled up, looked, rubbed my eyes, and, I believe, must have said something. The next thing I knew was that I was lying face downward on the road, with Kitty kneeling above me in tears.

'Has it gone, child?' I gasped. Kitty only wept more bitterly.

'Has what gone, Jack dear? What does it all mean? There must be a mistake somewhere, Jack. A hideous mistake.' Her last words brought me to my feet—mad—raving for the time being.

'Yes, there *is* a mistake somewhere,' I repeated, 'a hideous mistake. Come and look at It.'

I have an indistinct idea that I dragged Kitty by the wrist along the road up to where It stood, and implored her for pity's sake to speak to It; to tell It that we were betrothed; that neither Death nor Hell could break the tie between us: and Kitty only knows how much more to the same effect. Now and again I appealed passionately to the Terror in the 'rickshaw to bear witness to all I had said, and to release me from a torture that was killing me. As I talked I suppose I must have told Kitty of my old relations with Mrs Wessington, for I saw her listen intently with a white face and blazing eyes.

'Thank you, Mr Pansay,' she said, 'that's *quite* enough. Syce, *ghora lao.*'

The syces, impassive as Orientals always are, had come up

with the recaptured horses; and as Kitty sprang into her saddle I caught hold of her bridle, entreating her to hear me out and forgive. My answer was the cut of her riding-whip across my face from mouth to eye, and a word or two of farewell that even now I cannot write down. So I judged and judged rightly, that Kitty knew all; and I staggered back to the side of the 'rickshaw. My face was cut and bleeding, and the blow of the riding-whip had raised a livid blue wheal on it. I had no self-respect. Just then, Heatherlegh, who must have been following Kitty and me at a distance, cantered up.

'Doctor,' I said, pointing to my face, 'here's Miss Mannering's signature to my order of dismissal and I'll thank you for that lakh as soon as convenient.'

Heatherlegh's face, even in my abject miser, moved me to laughter.

'I'll stake my professional reputation' he began.

'Don't be a fool,' I whispered. 'I've lost my life's happiness and you'd better take me home.'

As I spoke the 'rickshaw was gone. Then I lost all knowledge of what was passing. The crest of Jakko seemed to heave and roll like the crest of a cloud and fall in upon me.

Seven days later (on the 7th of May, that is to say) I was aware that I was lying in Heatherlegh's room as weak as a little child. Heatherlegh was watching me intently from behind the papers on his writing-table. His first words were not encouraging; but I was too far spent to be much moved by them.

'Here's Miss Kitty has sent back your letters. You corresponded a good deal, you young people. Here's a packet that looks like a ring and a cheerful sort of a note from Mannering Papa, which I've taken the liberty of reading and burning. The old gentleman's not pleased with you.'

'And Kitty?' I asked dully.

'Rather more drawn than her father from what she says. By the same token you must have been letting out any number of queer reminiscences just before I met you. Says that a man who would have behaved to a woman as you did to Mrs Wessington ought to kill himself out of sheer pity for his kind. She's a hot-headed little virago, your mash. Will have it too that you were suffering from D.T. when that row on the Jakko road turned up. Says she'll die before she ever speaks to you again.'

I groaned and turned over on the other side.

'Now you've got your choice, my friend. This engagement has to be broken off; and the Mannerings don't want to be too hard on you. Was it broken through D.T. or epileptic fits? Sorry I can't offer you a better exchange unless you'd prefer hereditary insanity. Say the word and I'll tell 'em it's fits. All Simla knows about that scene on the Ladies' Mile. Come! I'll give you five minutes to think over it.'

During those five minutes I believe that I explored thoroughly the lowest circles of the inferno which man is permitted to tread on earth. And at the same time I was watching myself faltering through the dark labyrinths of doubt, misery and utter despair. I wondered, as Heatherlegh in his chair might have wondered, which dreadful alternative I should adopt. Presently I heard myself answering in a voice that I hardly recognized—

'They're confoundedly particular about morality in these parts. Give 'em fits, Heatherlegh, and my love. Now let me sleep a bit longer.'

Then my two selves joined, and it was only I (half-crazed, devil-driven I) that tossed in my bed tracing step by step the history of the past month.

'But I am in Simla,' I kept repeating to myself. 'I, Jack Pansay am in Simla, and there are no ghosts here. It's unreasonable of that woman to pretend there are. Why couldn't Agnes have left me alone? I never did her any harm. It might just as well have been me as Agnes. Only I'd never have come back on purpose to kill *her*. Why can't I be left alone—left alone and happy?'

It was high noon when I first awoke: and the sun was low in the sky before I slept—slept as the tortured criminal sleeps on his rack, too worn to feel further pain.

Next day I could not leave my bed. Heatherlegh told me in the morning that he had received an answer from Mr Mannering, and that, thanks to his (Heatherlegh's) friendly offices, the story of my affliction had travelled through the length and breadth of Simla, where I was on all sides much pitied.

'And that's rather more than you deserve,' he concluded pleasantly, 'though the Lord knows you've been going through a pretty severe mill. Never mind; we'll cure you yet, you perverse phenomenon.'

I declined firmly to be cured. 'You've been much too good to me already, old man,' said I; 'but I don't think I need trouble you further.'

In my heart I knew that nothing Heatherlegh could do would lighten the burden that had been laid upon me.

With that knowledge came also a sense of hopeless, impotent rebellion against the unreasonableness of it all. There were scores of men no better than I whose punishments had at least been reserved for another world; and I felt that it was bitterly, cruelly unfair that I alone should have been singled out for so hideous a fate. This mood would in time give place to another where it seemed that the 'rickshaw and I were the only realities in a world of shadows; that Kitty was a ghost; that Mannering, Heatherlegh, and all the other men and women I knew were all ghosts; and the great, gray hills themselves but vain shadows devised to torture me. From mood to mood I tossed backwards and forwards for seven weary days; my body growing daily stronger and stronger, until the bedroom looking-glass told me that I had returned to everyday life, and was as other men once more. Curiously enough my face showed no signs of the struggle I had gone through. It was pale indeed, but as expressionless and commonplace as ever. I had expected some permanent alteration—visible evidence of the disease that was eating me away. I found nothing.

On the 15th of May, I left Heatherlegh's house at eleven o'clock in the morning; and the instinct of the bachelor drove me to the club. There I found that every man knew my story as told by Heatherlegh, and was, in clumsy fashion, abnormally kind and attentive. Nevertheless, I recognized that for the rest of my natural life I should be among but not of my fellows; and I envied very bitterly indeed the laughing coolies on the Mall below. I lunched at the club, and at four o'clock wandered aimlessly down the Mall in the vague hope of meeting Kitty. Close to the Bandstand the black and white liveries joined me; and I heard Mrs Wessington's old appeal at my side. I had been expecting this ever since I came out; and was only surprised at her delay. The phantom 'rickshaw and I went side by side along the Chota Simla road in silence. Close to the bazar, Kitty and a man on horseback overtook and passed us. For any sign she gave I might have been a dog in the road. She did not even pay me the compliment of quickening her pace; though the rainy afternoon had served for an excuse.

So Kitty and her companion, and I and my ghostly Light-o'-Love, crept round Jakko in couples. The road was streaming with water; the pines dripped like roof-pipes on the rocks below, and the air was full of fine, driving rain. Two or three times I found myself saying to myself almost aloud: 'I'm Jack Pansay on leave at Simla—*at Simla!* Everyday, ordinary Simla. I mustn't forget that—I mustn't forget that.' Then I would try to recollect some of the gossip I had heard at the Club: the prices of so-and-so's horses—anything, in fact, that related to the work-a-day Anglo-Indian world I knew so well. I even repeated the multiplication-table rapidly to myself, to make quite sure that I was not taking leave of my senses. It gave me much comfort; and must have prevented my hearing Mrs Wessington for a time.

Once more I wearily climbed the Convent slope and entered the level road. Here Kitty and the man started off at a canter, and I was left alone with Mrs Wessington. 'Agnes,' said I, 'will you put back your hood and tell me what it all means?' The hood dropped noiselessly, and I was face to face with my dead and buried mistress. She was wearing the dress in which I had last seen her alive; carried the same tiny handkerchief in her right hand; and the same card-case in her left. (A woman eight months dead with a card-case!) I had to pin myself down to the multiplication-table, and to set both hands on the stone parapet of the road, to assure myself that that at least was real.

'Agnes,' I repeated, 'for pity's sake tell me what it all means.' Mrs Wessington leaned forward, with that odd, quick turn of the head I used to know so well, and spoke.

If my story had not already so madly overleaped the bounds of all human belief I should apologize to you now. As I know that no one—no, not even Kitty, for whom it is written as some sort of justification of my conduct—will believe me, I will go on. Mrs Wessington spoke and I walked with her from the Sanjowlie road to the turning below the Commander-in-Chief's house as I might walk by the side of any living woman's 'rickshaw, deep in conversation. The second and most tormenting of my moods of sickness had suddenly laid hold upon me, and like the prince in Tennyson's poem, 'I seemed to move amid a world of ghosts'. There had been a garden-party at the Commander-in-Chief's, and we two joined the crowd of homeward-bound folk. As I saw them it seemed that *they* were the shadows—impalpable fantastic shadows—that divided for Mrs Wessington's 'rickshaw to pass through. What we said during the course of that weird interview I cannot—indeed, I dare not—tell. Heatherlegh's comment would have been a short laugh and a remark that I had been 'mashing a brain-eye-and-stomach chimera'. It was a ghastly and, yet in some indefinable way, a marvellously dear experience. Could it be possible, I wondered, that I was in this life to woo a second time the woman I had killed by my own neglect and cruelty?

I met Kitty on the homeward road—a shadow among shadows. If I were to describe all the incidents of the next fortnight in their order, my story would never come to an end; and your patience would be exhausted. Morning after morning and evening after evening the ghostly 'rickshaw and I used to wander through Simla together. Wherever I went the four black and white liveries followed me and bore me company to and from my hotel. At the theatre I found them amid the crowd of yelling jhampanies; outside the club verandah, after a long evening of whist; at the Birthday Ball, waiting patiently for my reappearance; and in broad daylight when I went calling. Save that it cast no shadow, the 'rickshaw was in every respect as real to look upon as one of wood and iron. More than once, indeed, I have had to check myself from warning some hard-riding friend against cantering over it. More than once I have walked down the Mall deep in conversation with Mrs Wessington to the unspeakable amazement of the passers-by.

Before I had been out and about a week I learned that the 'fit' theory had been discarded in favour of insanity. However, I made no change in my mode of life. I called, rode, and dined out as freely as ever. I had a passion for the society of my kind which I had never felt before; I hungered to be among the realities of

NIGHT OF THE MILLENNIUM

Ruskin Bond

Jackals howled dismally, foraging for bones and offal down in the khud below the butcher's shop. Pasand was unperturbed by the sound. A robust young computer whiz-kid and patriotic multinational, he prided himself on being above and beyond all superstitious fears of the unknown. In his lexicon, the unknown was just something that was waiting to be discovered. Hence this walk, past the old cemetery late at night.

Midnight would see the new millennium in. The year 2000 beckoned, full of bright prospects for well-heeled young men like Pasand. True, there were millions—soon to be over a billion—sweating it out in the heat and dust of the plains below, scraping together a meagre living for themselves and their sprawling families. Not for them the advantages of a public school education, three cars in the garage, and a bank account in Bermuda. Ah well, mused Pasand, not everyone could have the brains and good luck, as well as inherited family wealth of course, that had made life so pleasant and promising for him. This was going to be the century in which the smart-asses would get to the top and all other varieties of asses would sink to the bottom. It was important to have a ruling elite, according to his philosophy; only then could slaves prosper!

He looked at his watch. It was just past midnight. He had eaten well, and he was enjoying his little walk along the lonely winding road which took him past the houses of the rich and famous, the Lais, the Banerjees, the Kapoors, the Ramchandanis— he was as good as any of them! Better, in fact. He was approaching his own personal Everest, while they had reached theirs and were on the downward slope, or so he presumed.

Here was the cemetery with its broken old tombstones, some of them dating from a hundred and fifty years ago: pathetic reminders of a once-powerful empire, now reduced to dust and crumbling monuments. Here lay colonels and magistrates, merchants and memsahibs, and many small children; fragile lives which had been snuffed out in more turbulent times. To Pasand, they were losers, all of them. He had nothing but contempt for those who hadn't been able to hang on to their power and glory. No lost empires for him!

The road here was very dark, for the trees grew thick on the northern slopes. Pasand felt a twinge of nervousness, but he was reassured by the feel of the cellphone in his pocket—he could always summon his driver or his armed bodyguard to come and pick him up.

The moon had risen over Nag Tibba, and the graves stood out in serried rows, as though forming a guard of honour for this modern knight in T-shirt and designer jeans. Through the deodars he saw a faint light on the perimeter of the cemetery. Here, he had learnt from one of his chamchas, lived a widow with a brood of small children. Although in poor health, she was still young and comely, and known to be lavish with her favours to those who were generous with their purses; for she needed the money for her hungry family.

She was also a little mad, they said, and preferred to sleep in one of the old domed tombs rather than in the quarters provided for her late husband, who had been the caretaker.

This did not bother Pasand. He was in search of sensual pleasure, not romance. And right now he felt an urgent need to exert his dominance over someone, preferably a woman, for he had to prove his manhood in some way. So far, most young women had shied away from his vainglorious and clumsy approach.

This woman wasn't young. She was in her late thirties, and poverty, malnutrition and ill-use had made her look much older. But there were vestiges of beauty in her smouldering eyes and sinewy limbs. Her gypsy blood must have had something to do with it. Her teeth gleamed in the darkness as she smiled at Pasand and invited him into her boudoir—the spacious tomb that she favoured most.

Pasand had no time for tender love-play. Clumsily, he clawed at her breasts but found they were not much larger than his own. He tore at her already tattered clothes, pressed his mouth hungrily to her dry lips. She made no attempt to resist. He had his way. Then, while he lay supine across the cold damp slab of a grave that covered the remains of some long-dead warrior, she leaned over him and bit him on the cheek and neck.

He cried out in pain and astonishment, and tried to sit up. But a number of hands, small but strong, thrust him back against the tombstone. Small mouths, sharp teeth, pressed against his flesh. Muddy fingers tore at his clothes. Those young teeth bit—and bit again. His screams mingled with the cries of the jackals.

'Patience, my children, patience,' crooned the woman. 'There is more than enough for all of you.'

They feasted.

Down in the ravine, the jackals started howling again, awaiting their turn. The bones would be theirs. Only the cellphone would be rejected.

THE MIRROR

Reeta Dutta Gupta

Outside, in the fresh green lawn at 7 Chowrangee Street, Ruby was playing a game of her own. And along the edges of the green grass, white lilies and tuberoses bloomed. So did sweet-smelling jasmines on the trailing creeper. The monsoon had arrived. Among the white flowers, creamish, powder-puff butterflies flitted about when the rains took a rest.

Sitting on the windowsill, inhaling the perfumed air, Anjoli watched her little sister. She was always playing games. Little brat! How Mom indulged in her whims and fancies! And what a wild imagination she had! 'I can see ghosts,' she often said with a straight face. Liar! It sometimes worried Mom and Dad. But, they laughed it off. The other day, when Ruby and Anjoli stood out after dinner in their garden in the silver moonlight, to have a moonlight bath—which Ruby said was better than sunbathing in the hot, humid climate of Calcutta—she suddenly looked up into the dark terrace streaked with faint moonbeams.

'There's aunty up there on the terrace, standing all alone in the moonlight,' Ruby had said. 'She is looking at us.'

Aunty was Dad's only sister. Only a year ago she had died of cancer.

How frightened Anjoli was that night! Mom and Dad were away at a party to which children were not invited. Why not? Wondered Anjoli. She was fifteen, going on sixteen and she loved to *go* to parties. Dress up. Put on her light blue chiffon dress embroidered with little white pearls and sequins. Mom had given her that beautiful dress on her fifteenth birthday, only a month ago. And the ornate dresser with a beautiful mirror, which had inlay work with mother-of-pearl along the edges, was a gift from Dad.

'Aunty is calling us,' Ruby had persisted as she stared into the empty space with her eyes and followed the movement of someone walking about.

'What utter nonsense,' Anjoli had snapped back, putting up a brave face. She didn't want to let her sister discover how afraid she was when she spoke like that. For instance, on her birthday, when she was most happy, Ruby had told her just before going to bed, 'He'll come!'

'Who'll come?... What on earth are you talking about?' Anjoli had asked, pinching her sister's chubby cheek so firmly that it left a red patch on her smooth fair skin. That serves her right for making me worry, she thought.

But Ruby had screamed into her ears, her eyes round like two white-and-black marbles, 'Of course, he will! Don't you believe me?'

The next morning, when Anjoli told her mother about the strange things Ruby had been telling her, her mother kept her cool.

At least, she pretended to look all right. And she even sided with the baby of the house.

'She is seven years younger to you, Ann. Why do you take everything she says so seriously? Children of her age play games like that. They live in a world of their own.'

Anjoli said nothing but felt a little hurt and angry inside. Her mother was always taking her sister's side. Spoilt child! Wasn't she glad that evening when Dad had chided Ruby as he was helping Anjoli solve a mathematical problem and Ruby came yelling into the room. 'He'll come! He'll come!'

Dad had sharply said, 'That's enough, Ruby! Mom has been telling me about all the naughty things you say! Have you not heard the story "Cry Wolf"? If you go on pretending, no one will believe you. Now, don't make a noise here, your Didi is studying.'

Days and weeks had passed since that evening. Almost a month was over. Ruby was away at her Grandma's house for the weekend and Anjoli was glad for that. She could now have her Mom all to herself for two days, thought Anjoli. Not that she didn't like going to Grandma's, but monthly tests were round the corner. So, she sat at her desk studying, when the doorbell rang. A short buzz, followed by a long, impatient ring. It had been drizzling outside, which turned into a shower. Anjoli could hear the pitter-patter of rain.

Anjoli's mother was busy at her computer. She worked for an Internet company and was always very busy. Her Dad, too, was busy with his clients discussing legal matters. So, Anjoli got up to answer the doorbell. Opening the door she saw a man, a little away from the entrance. The gentleman wore a white shirt and a pair of neatly pressed white trousers. His hair was completely silver like moonlight. He was thin and frail. Anjoli thought he looked like a stick of tuberose plucked from the garden outside. But how did he come in through the rain? He didn't have an umbrella. The man half-smiled.

'Yes?' Anjoli asked.

At first the man didn't say a word but continued to stare at Anjoli for sometime. Anjoli blinked and stared back. He didn't look happy. He seemed to have a sad countenance.

'Have you come to see Dad?' Anjoli asked looking away from the man as if trying hard to break away from the hold of his stare.

'It's the mirror,' the man said at length, almost in a whisper. I've come for it. Could I please have it back? The mirror you had bought a month ago from The Roy's Auction Mart at Freeschool Street? You see, it belonged to me. I'd no intention of putting it up for the sale. There was some mistake about it.'

Anjoli was horrified. She had grown much too fond of her mirror to part with it. She quickly looked back over her shoulders. Thank god, her parents were unaware they had a visitor. Thank god, Ruby was away. She would never come to know about this man and tattle about it to her mother. Anjoli had no intention of parting with the mirror. She was just discovering the world of teenage cosmetics and junk jewellery. She loved to look pretty for she had a feeling deep inside her—which no one knew—that she was not as good-looking as her little sister. So when she was not studying, she spent time before the mirror doing her make-up, combing her hair this way and that way and generally fussing over her looks.

In a hushed voice, she quickly replied, 'Ah, well! But I think it was sold to us. We'd bought it. You see, it was my birthday present.'

The man shook his head resolutely.

Anjoli shrugged up her shoulders. 'I'm sorry,' she said and before the man could say another word, she shut the door.

A week passed. Anjoli kept the visit of the man a closely guarded secret. She almost forgot about it. Then, one evening, when Ruby and she sat on the windowsill listening to the wind making strange noises among the palm fronds just outside their garden—for it had begun to drizzle and they couldn't go out for a stroll—Ruby suddenly stood up, closed her eyes and in a low whisper said, 'He's on his way. That man in white.'

Anjoli's heart missed a beat. Suddenly, she remembered the man who had come asking for her mirror. Of course, Ruby had told her, 'He'll come.' And now she was saying, 'That man in white.' How did Ruby know so much? Perhaps, her sister was not playing any game after all. There was something real about what she said. There was something uncanny about her that made her afraid. Was she what people called a clairvoyant? Was that the word, which meant a person who knew things in advance? Anjoli had read about it in a storybook.

For the first time giving her sister a measure of importance, Anjoli asked, testing her sister, 'How do you know he's on his way?'

'I know. I can see. He'll be back,' Ruby said.

'He'll be back—what do you mean?' Anjoli asked.

Ruby shrugged her shoulders and looked nonchalant.

Anjoli's heart began to pound. 'Tell me, why should he come?' she demanded. Ruby burst out laughing. 'Of course, you know! Don't pretend to be an angel.'

Anjoli held her breath, trying hard not to look too anxious as she continued with her interrogation, 'Tell me what else do you see?'

'I see him coming. I see him coming,' Ruby said closing her eyes and sniffing the air like a police dog.

'What makes you sniff the air, stupid?' Anjoli said.

'I can smell something like dad's eau-de-cologne. Now it is right in this room,' Ruby said, opening her eyes. 'Why, there he is!' she exclaimed.

Anjoli stared at her sister, totally bewildered. 'Where is he?' she whispered.

'He is in your mirror,' she said. 'He is not looking at me.

He is looking at you.'

Anjoli was terrified. But, nonetheless, she managed to say, 'Nonsense. What utter nonsense!' giving a quick sidelong glance at the mirror. But there was nothing that she saw. She was sure, Ruby was playing—just playing a game. But how did she know about the man in white? Was it all a coincidence?

Thank god! The children's mother walked into the room just then. 'Ann and Ruby, dinner time!' she announced.

Anjoli wanted to run to her and hold her hand. But before she could get up—her legs were shaking—Ruby followed her mother out. Then, just as Anjoli was about to leave the room, a wind rose and a blast came in through the window. With a howl it banged the door shut. And just then, there was a flash of lightning in the sky. And a faint smell of men's cologne filled the room. Anjoli's heart began to race. She nervously glanced at the mirror and her heart missed a beat. Goodness gracious! There he was! That man in white. Staring hard at Anjoli. He looked displeased. Rather annoyed. Anjoli stumbled and fell and somehow managed to catch hold of the doorknob—it felt slippery and very cold; the room temperature too seemed to take a sudden dip—and opening the door, ran out and fell straight onto her Dad's lap.

'What's the matter, Ann? Why, you're perspiring?' the doting father asked, stroking his daughter's hair. Turning to Ruby, he chided her, 'Have you been frightening your sister, Ruby? Lying again?'

Now, for the first time Anjoli came to the rescue of her little sister. 'Ruby's not lying Dad. He is there—in the mirror! I saw him! There's a man in the mirror!'

Mr and Mrs Bannerji were speechless. They exchanged a long worried look. What was wrong with their girls? Were they reading too many nonsense tales? Too many ghost stories?

Mrs Bannerji, who sat frozen on her chair, was truly perturbed. 'This has been going on for sometime. First, Ruby said she saw him. And now Anjoli. Look at their faces!'

'And look at your face, ma'am,' Mr Bannerji smiled, addressing his wife. To lighten the situation he jokingly added. 'Are you going to say, too, that there's a man in Anjoli's mirror?'

Mr Bannerji laughed.

Mrs Bannerji laughed too. But her face was as pale as her girls were for she could sense the terror in Ann's heart. And that look of certainty on Ruby's face gave her the shivers. At once, she sent her husband to the children's room to check it out himself. This act she was sure, would pacify her eldest daughter.

'Why, I see nothing. Nobody's in here, silly girls!' called back Mr Bannerji. He shut the door and came over shaking his head. 'How absurd can you all get?'

'Well girls, that settles it! There's no one there,' Mrs Bannerji said with visible relief.

But Anjoli insisted, 'I'm going to sleep with you, Mom! He's there in my mirror!'

'Tonight, you may sleep with us. Both of you. But tomorrow, I don't want anymore stories,' Mrs Bannerji reproved.

'But tomorrow, he isn't going to go away,' Ruby said with a straight face.

Anjoli gasped.

Mr Bannerji pretended to ignore the children and began to eat. Mrs Bannerji looked nervous.

That night, when the children fell asleep, Mr Bannerji said, 'We must consul Dr R.K. Majumdar. He's the best child psychologist in the city. I'm beginning to get really worried.'

'My daughters are not mad,' Mrs Bannerji protested. 'You never know with antique stuff,' his wife stated. 'I think you'd better sell if off. I don't want it in my house. A mirror like that, anyone will want to buy.'

Mr Bannerji sighed.

The next day, Anjoli avoided going to her room. Ruby fetched her sister's clothes and schoolbooks from her desk and Anjoli did her homework sitting in the dining room. It was Sunday, and after weeks the sky didn't pour. In the afternoon, Anjoli and Ruby went for a walk in the park. And guess whom they met? Mr Roy, the man who auctioned old furniture.

He called out. 'There you are Anjoli! Your father was there to see me this morning. He told me he was looking for a buyer for the mirror. Why, did you not like it? I've an antique three-legged table made of the finest teak. It came this evening. Would your father be interested?' he asked.

Anjoli was sad to hear that the mirror would now be sold off. However, she asked with growing curiosity, 'Where did you get that mirror from?'

'A lovely piece, isn't it? Exquisite, I'd say! Won't find another anywhere in India,' Mr Roy said.

Was the man deaf? Anjoli raised her voice, 'But where did you get it from, uncle?'

'It must be a hundred years old,' Mr Roy beamed.

'A hundred years old?' Anjoli exclaimed.

'Yes, a hundred years old. It belonged to Mr John's mother. She gave it to her daughter-in-law, Betty John, the beautiful lady of Park Circus. I'd always had an eye on it. John had been selling their old articles to me for many years. But he wouldn't agree to parting with the mirror, even after Mrs John died a couple of years ago. John said, "My mother was fond of it. My wife was fond of it. Betty spent hours at it doing up her lovely hair and make-up." But last year, when John died, a distant relation of theirs sold off all their possessions and their house. That's how I got the mirror. You've got it now, but your father doesn't want it suddenly. Why?' Mr Roy asked grinning at Anjoli. He was an aged man and had endearing ways.

'We know him! It's Mr John who is in our mirror!' Ruby suddenly blabbered.

'What, what?' Mr Roy asked looking curiously at the girl. 'Is she your sister?' he asked, and pointing his thin bony finger to his head he indicated that all was not right with her head.

Anjoli quickly turned her back and walked back home clutching Ruby's hand. 'Goodbye, uncle,' she called out.

That very evening the Bannerjis had visitors. A young man and his wife rang the doorbell and were ushered in straight to the children's bedroom.

'This is the mirror and the dressing-table for sale,' Mr Bannerji said.

'How beautiful!' the woman exclaimed.

Anjoli wanted to cry. She loved the mirror but was afraid of it. Standing at the door, she cast a quick sideways glance at it. Why, there was no one in it. Was it then her wild imagination? It was raining cats and dogs that awful night when she thought she saw him in it. The sky was drumming with thunder. The wind was tearing at the tops of the tress. In a situation like that one was bound to imagine things. Or, was it because of Ruby's influence? After all, if someone kept telling you stories and acted and behaved in the strange way she did, you were bound to be affected by it, thought Anjoli. Naughty girl! Because of Ruby, she was going to lose her mirror. An awful feeling of loss and sadness came over Anjoli. Then, she suddenly recalled the man in white who had actually come asking for the mirror. Anjoli had to admit that there was some mystery in it, after all.

With a sigh, Anjoli gave one last glance at the mirror as it was carted away. How beautiful it was! Suddenly, to her horror, Mr John's face appeared in it. His hair shining like moonlight.

His eyes blazing. His skin as white as the lilies. Only Anjoli could see him. And Ruby, who came in just then, stopped dead. The children screamed, 'There is Mr John!'

Mr Bannerji smiled with embarrassment at the man and the woman who looked puzzled. Then, suddenly, a loud smash, like glass breaking, came from the mirror. An awful sound it was! As if someone had got into a fit of rage and was pounding glass. And then, to everyone's horror, the mirror cracked.

The mirror, the lovely mirror, would never be of use to anyone anymore. It could never be anyone's mirror, except Mrs John's. Mr John had made sure of that.

THE BEAST WITH FIVE FINGERS

W.F. Harvey

The story, I suppose, begins with Adrian Borlsover, whom I met when I was a little boy and he an old man. My father had called to appeal for a subscription, and before he left, Mr Borlsover laid his right hand in blessing on my head. I shall never forget the awe in which I gazed up at his face and realized for the first time that eyes might be dark and beautiful and shining, and yet not able to see.

For Adrian Borlsover was blind.

He was an extraordinary man, who came of an eccentric stock. Borlsover sons for some reason always seemed to marry very ordinary women, which perhaps accounted for the fact that no Borlsover had been a genius, and only one Borlsover had been mad. But they were great champions of little causes, generous patrons of odd sciences, founders of querulous sects, trustworthy guides to the bypath meadows of erudition.

Adrian was an authority on the fertilization of orchids. He had held at one time the family living at Borlsover Conyers, until a congenital weakness of the lungs obliged him to seek a less rigorous climate in the sunny south-coast watering-place where I had seen him. Occasionally, he would relieve one or other of the local clergy. My father described him as a fine preacher, who gave long and inspiring sermons from what many men would have considered unprofitable texts. 'An excellent proof,' he would add, 'of the truth of the doctrine of direct verbal inspiration.'

Adrian Borlsover was exceedingly clever with his hands. His penmanship was exquisite. He illustrated all his scientific papers, made his own woodcuts, and carved the reredos that is at present the chief feature of interest in the church at Borlsover Conyers. He had an exceedingly clever knack in cutting silhouettes for young ladies and paper pigs and cows for little children, and made more than one complicated wind instrument of his own devising.

When he was fifty years old, Adrian Borlsover lost his sight. In a wonderfully short time he adapted himself to the new conditions of life. He quickly learnt to read Braille. So marvellous indeed was his sense of touch, that he was still able to maintain his interest in botany. The mere passing of his long supple fingers over a flower was sufficient means for its identification, though occasionally he would use his lips. I have found several letters of his among my father's correspondence; in no case was there anything to show that he was afflicted with blindness, and this in spite of the fact that he exercised undue economy in the spacing of lines. Towards the close of his life, Adrian Borlsover was credited with the powers of touch that seemed almost uncanny. It has been said that he could tell at once the colour of a ribbon placed between his fingers. My father would neither confirm nor deny the story.

Adrian Borlsover was a bachelor. His elder brother, Charles, had married late in life, leaving one son, Eustace, who lived in the gloomy Georgian mansion at Borlsover Conyers, where he could work undisturbed in collecting material for his great book on heredity.

Like his uncle, he was a remarkable man. The Borlsovers had always been born naturalists, but Eustace possessed in a special degree the power of systematizing his knowledge. He had received his university education in Germany; and then, after post-graduate work in Vienna and Naples, had travelled for four years in South America and the East, getting together a huge store of material for a new study into the processes of variation.

He lived alone at Borlsover Conyers with Saunders, his secretary, a man who bore a somewhat dubious reputation in the district, but whose powers as a mathematician, combined with his business abilities, were invaluable to Eustace.

Uncle and nephew saw little of each other. The visits of Eustace were confined to a week in the summer or autumn—tedious weeks, that dragged almost as slowly as the bath-chair in which the old man was drawn along the sunny sea-front. In their way the two men were fond of each other, though their intimacy would, doubtless, have been greater, had they shared the same religious views. Adrian held to the old-fashioned evangelical dogmas of his early manhood; his nephew for many years had been thinking of embracing Buddhism. Both men possessed, too, the reticence the Borlsovers had always shown, and which their enemies sometimes called hypocrisy. With Adrian it was a reticence as to the things he had left undone; but with Eustace it seemed that the curtain which he was so careful to leave undrawn hid something more than a half-empty chamber.

Two years before his death, Adrian Borlsover developed, unknown to himself, the not uncommon power of automatic writing. Eustace made the discovery by accident. Adrian was sitting reading in bed, the forefinger of his left hand tracing the Braille characters, when his nephew noticed that a pencil the old man held in his right hand was moving slowly along the opposite page. He left his seat in the window and sat down beside the bed. The right hand continued to move, and now he could see plainly that they were letters and words which it was forming.

'Adrian Borlsover,' wrote the hand, 'Eustace Borlsover, Charles Borlsover, Francis Borlsover, Sigismund Borlsover, Adrian Borlsover, Eustace Borlsover, Saville Borlsover. B for Borlsover. Honesty is the Best Policy. Beautiful Belinda Borlsover.'

'What curious nonsense!' said Eustace to himself.

'King George ascended the throne in 1760,' wrote the hand. 'Crowd, a noun of multitude; a collection of individuals. Adrian Borlsover, Eustace Borlsover.'

'It seems to me,' said his uncle, closing the book, 'that you had much better make the most of the afternoon sunshine and take your walk now.'

'I think perhaps I will,' Eustace answered as he picked up the volume. 'I won't go far, and when I come back, I can read to you those articles in *Nature* about which we were speaking.'

He went along the promenade, but stopped at the first shelter, and, seating himself in the corner best protected from the wind, he examined the book at leisure. Nearly every page was scored with a meaningless jumble of pencil-marks; rows of capital letters, short words, long words, complete sentences, copy-book tags. The whole thing, in fact had the appearance of a copy-book, and, on a more careful scrutiny, Eustace thought that there was ample evidence to show that the handwriting at the beginning of the book, good though it was, was not nearly so good as the handwriting at the end.

He left his uncle at the end of October with a promise to return early in December. It seemed to him quite clear that the old man's power of automatic writing was developing rapidly, and for the first time he looked forward to a visit that would combine duty with interest.

But on his return he was at first disappointed. His uncle, he thought, looked older. He was listless, too, preferring others to read to him and dictating nearly all his letters. Not until the day before he left had Eustace an opportunity of observing Adrian Borlsover's new-found faculty.

The old man, propped up in bed with pillows, had sunk into a light sleep. His two hands lay on the coverlet, his left hand tightly clasping his right. Eustace took an empty manuscript-book and placed a pencil within reach of the fingers of the right hand. They snatched at it eagerly, then dropped the pencil to loose the left hand from its restraining grasp.

'Perhaps to prevent interference I had better hold that hand,' said Eustace to himself, as he watched the pencil. Almost immediately it began to write.

'Blundering Borlsovers, unnecessarily unnatural, extraordinarily eccentric, culpably curious.'

'Who are you?' asked Eustace in a low voice.

'Never you mind,' wrote the hand of Adrian.

'Is it my uncle who is writing?'

'O my prophetic soul, mine uncle!'

'Is it anyone I know?'

'Silly Eustace, you'll see me very soon.'

'When shall I see you?'

'When poor old Adrian's dead.'

'Where shall I see you?'

'Where shall you not?'

Instead of speaking his next question, Eustace wrote it. 'What is the time?'

The fingers dropped the pencil and moved three or four times across the paper. Then, picking up the pencil, they wrote: 'Ten minutes before four. Put your book away, Eustace. Adrian mustn't find us working at this sort of thing. He doesn't know what to make of it, and I won't have poor old Adrian disturbed. Au revoir!'

Adrian Borlsover awoke with a start.

'I've been dreaming again,' he said; 'such queer dreams of leaguered cities and forgotten towns. You were mixed up in this one, Eustace, though I can't remember how. Eustace, I want to warn you. Don't walk in doubtful paths. Choose your friends well. Your poor grandfather...'

A fit of coughing put an end to what he was saying, but Eustace saw that the hand was still writing. He managed unnoticed to draw the book away. 'I'll light the gas,' he said, 'and ring for tea.' On the other side of the bed-curtain he saw the last sentences that had been written.

'It's too late, Adrian,' he read. 'We're friends already, aren't we, Eustace Borlsover?'

On the following day Eustace left. He thought his uncle looked ill when he said goodbye, and the old man spoke despondently of the failure his life had been.

'Nonsense, uncle,' said his nephew. 'You have got over your difficulties in a way not one in a hundred thousand would have done. Everyone marvels at your splendid perseverance in teaching your hand to take the place of your lost sight. To me it's been a revelation of the possibilities of education.'

'Education,' said his uncle dreamily, as if the word had started a new train of thought. 'Education is good so long as you know to whom and for what purpose you give it. But with the lower orders of men, the base and more sordid spirits, I have grave doubts as to its results. Well, goodbye, Eustace; I may not see you again. You are a true Borlsover, with all the Borlsover faults. Marry, Eustace. Marry some good, sensible girl. And if by any chance I don't see you again, my will is at my solicitor's. I've not left you any legacy, because I know you're well-provided for; but I thought you might like to have my books. Oh, and there's just one other thing. You know, before the end people often lose control over themselves and make absurd requests. Don't pay any attention to them, Eustace. Goodbye!' and he held out his hand. Eustace took it. It remained in his a fraction of a second longer than he had expected and gripped him with a virility that was surprising. There was, too, in its touch a subtle sense of intimacy.

'Why, uncle,' he said, 'I shall see you alive and well for many long years to come.'

Two months later Adrian Borlsover died.

Eustace Borlsover was in Naples at the time. He read the obituary notice in the *Morning Post* on the day announced for the funeral.

'Poor old fellow!' he said. 'I wonder whether I shall find room for all his books.'

The question occurred to him again with greater force when three days later, he found himself standing in the library at Borlsover Conyers, a huge room built for use and not for beauty in the year of Waterloo by a Borlsover who was an ardent admirer of the great Napoleon. It was arranged on the plan of many college libraries, with tall projecting bookcases forming deep recesses of dusty silence, fit graves for the old hates of forgotten controversy, the dead passions of forgotten lives. At the end of the room, behind the bust of some unknown eighteenth-century divine, an ugly iron corkscrew stair led to a shelf-lined gallery. Nearly, every shelf was full.

'I must talk to Saunders about it,' said Eustace. 'I suppose that we shall have to have the billiard-room fitted up with bookcases.'

The two men met for the first time after many weeks in

the dining-room that evening.

'Hallo!' said Eustace, standing before the fire with his hands in his pockets. 'How goes the world, Saunders? Why these dress togs?' He himself was wearing an old shooting-jacket. He did not believe in mourning, as he had told his uncle on his last visit; and, though he usually went in for quiet-coloured ties, he wore this evening one of an ugly red, in order to shock Morton, the butler, and to make them thrash out the whole question of mourning for themselves in the servants' hall. Eustace was a true Borlsover. 'The world,' said Saunders, 'goes the same as usual, confoundedly slow. The dress togs are accounted for by an invitation from Captain Lockwood to bridge.'

'How are you getting there?'

'There's something the matter with the car, so I've told Jackson to drive me round in the dogcart. Any objection?'

'O dear me, no! We've had all things in common for far too many years for me to raise objections at this hour of the day.'

'You'll find your correspondence in the library,' went on Saunders. 'Most of it I've seen to. There are a few private letters I haven't opened. There's also a box with a rat or something inside it that came by the evening post. Very likely it's the six-toed beast Terry was sending us to cross with the four-toed albino. I didn't look because I didn't want to mess up my things; but I should gather from the way it's jumping about that it's pretty hungry'

'Oh, I'll see to it,' said Eustace, 'while you and the captain earn an honest penny.'

Dinner over and Saunders gone, Eustace went into the library. Though the fire had been lit, the room was by no means cheerful.

'We'll have all the lights on, at any rate,' he said, as he turned the switches. 'And, Morton,' he added, when the butler brought the coffee, 'get me a screwdriver or something to undo this box. Whatever the animal is, he's kicking up the deuce of a row. What is it? Why are you dawdling?'

'If you please, sir, when the postman brought it, he told me that they'd bored the holes in the lid at the post office. There were no breathing holes in the lid, sir, and they didn't want the animal to die. That is all, sir.'

'It's culpably careless of the man, whoever he was,' said Eustace as he removed the screws, 'packing an animal like this in a wooden box with no means of getting air. Confound it all! I meant to ask Morton to bring me a cage to put it in. Now I suppose I shall have to get one myself.'

He placed a heavy book on the lid from which the screws had been removed, and went into the billiard-room. As he came back into the library with an empty cage in his hand, he heard the sound of something falling, and then of something scuttling along the floor.

'Bother it! The beast's got out. How in the world am I to find it again in this library?'

To search for it did indeed seem hopeless. He tried to follow the sound of the scuttling in one of the recesses, where the animal seemed to be running behind the books on the shelves; but it was impossible to locate it. Eustace resolved to go on quietly reading. Very likely the animal might gain confidence and show itself Saunders seemed to have dealt in his usual methodical manner with most of the correspondence. There were still the private letters.

What was that? Two sharp clicks and the lights in the hideous candelabra that hung from the ceiling suddenly went out.

'I wonder if something has gone wrong with the fuse,' said Eustace, as he went to the switches by the door. Then he stopped. There was a noise at the other end of the room, as if something was crawling up the iron corkscrew stair. 'If it's gone into the gallery,' he said, 'well and good.' He hastily turned on the lights, crossed the room, and climbed up the stair. But he could see nothing. His grandfather had placed a little gate at the top of the stair, so that children could run and romp in the gallery without fear of accident. This Eustace closed, and, having considerably narrowed the circle of his search, returned to his desk by the fire.

How gloomy the library was! There was no sense of intimacy about the room. The few busts that an eighteenth-century Borlsover had brought back from the grand tour might have been in keeping in the old library. Here they seemed out of place. They made the room feel cold in spite of the heavy red damask curtains and great gilt cornices.

With a crash two heavy books fell from the gallery to the floor; then, as Borlsover looked, another, and yet another.

'Very well. You'll starve for this, my beauty!' he said. 'We'll do some little experiments on the metabolism of rats deprived of water. Go on! Chuck them down! I think I've got the upper hand.' He turned once more to his correspondence. The letter was from the family solicitor. It spoke of his uncle's death, and of the valuable collection of books that had been left to him in the will.

'There was one request [he read] which certainly came as a surprise to me. As you know, Mr Adrian Borlsover had left instructions that his body was to be buried in as simple a manner as possible at Eastbourne. He expressed a desire that there should be neither wreaths nor flowers of any kind, and hoped that his friends and relatives would not consider it necessary to wear mourning. The day before his death we received a letter cancelling these instructions. He wished the body to be embalmed (he gave us the address of the man we were to employ—Pennifer, Ludgate Hill), with orders that his right hand should be sent to you stating that it was at your special request. The other arrangements about the funeral remained unaltered.'

'Good Lord,' said Eustace, 'what in the world was the old boy driving at? And what in the name of all that's holy is that?'

Someone was in the gallery. Someone had pulled the cord attached to one of the blinds, and it had rolled up with a snap. Someone must be in the gallery, for a second blind did the same. Someone must be walking round the gallery, for one after the other the blinds sprang up, letting in the moonlight.

'I haven't got to the bottom of this yet,' said Eustace, 'but I will do, before the night is very much older'; and he hurried up the corkscrew stair. He had just got to the top when the lights went out a second time, and he heard again the scuttling along the floor. Quickly he stole on tiptoe in the dim moonshine in the direction of the noise, feeling, as he went, for one of the switches. His fingers touched the metal knob at last. He turned on the electric light.

About ten yards in front of him, crawling along the floor, was a man's hand. Eustace stared at it in utter amazement. It was moving quickly in the manner of a geometer caterpillar, the fingers humped up one moment, flattened out the next; the thumb appeared to give a crablike motion all the while. While he was looking, too surprised to stir, the hand disappeared round the corner. Eustace ran forward. He no longer saw it, but he could hear it, as it squeezed its way behind the books on one of the shelves. A heavy volume had been displaced. There was a gap in the row of books, where it had got in. In his fear lest it should escape him again, he seized the first book that came to his hand and plugged it into the hole. Then, emptying two shelves of their contents, he took the wooden boards and propped them up in front to make his barrier doubly sure.

'I wish Saunders was back,' he said; 'one can't tackle this sort of thing alone.' It was after eleven, and there seemed little likelihood of Saunders returning before twelve. He did not dare to leave the shelf unwatched, even to run downstairs to ring the bell. Morton, the butler, often used to come round about eleven to see that the windows were fastened, but he might not come. Eustace was thoroughly unstrung. At last he heard steps down below.

'Morton!' he shouted. 'Morton!'

'Sir?'

'Has Mr Saunders got back yet?'

'Not yet, sir.'

'Well, bring me some brandy, and hurry up about it. I'm up in the gallery, you duffer.'

'Thanks,' said Eustace, as he emptied the glass. 'Don't go to bed yet, Morton. There are a lot of books that have fallen down by accident. Bring them up and put them back on their shelves.'

Morton had never seen Borlsover in so talkative a mood as on that night. 'Here,' said Eustace, when the books had been put back and dusted, 'you might hold up these boards for me, Morton. That beast in the box got out, and I've been chasing it all over the place.'

'I think I can hear it chewing at the books, sir. They're not valuable, I hope? I think that's the carriage, sir; I'll go and call Mr Saunders.'

It seemed to Eustace that he was away for five minutes, but it could hardly have been more than one, when he returned with Saunders. 'All right, Morton, you can go now. I'm up here, Saunders.'

'What's all the row?' asked Saunders, as he lounged forward

with his hands in his pockets. The luck had been with him all the evening. He was completely satisfied, both with himself and with Captain Lockwood's taste in wines. 'What's the matter? You look to me to be in an absolutely blue funk.'

'That old devil of an uncle of mine,' began Eustace—'Oh, I can't explain it all. It's his hand that's been playing Old Harry all the evening. But I've got it cornered behind these books. You've got to help me to catch it.'

'What's up with you, Eustace? What's the game?'

'It's no game, you silly idiot! If you don't believe me, take out one of those books and put your hand in and feel.'

'All right,' said Saunders; 'but wait till I've rolled up my sleeve. The accumulated dust of centuries, eh?' He took off his coat, knelt down, and thrust his arm along the shelf.

'There's something there right enough,' he said. 'It's got a funny, stumpy end to it, whatever it is, and nips like a crab. Ah! no, you don't!' He pulled his hand out in a flash. 'Shove in a book quickly. Now it can't get out.'

'What was it?' asked Eustace.

'Something that wanted very much to get hold of me. I felt what seemed like a thumb and forefinger. Give me some brandy.'

'How are we to get it out of there?'

'What about a landing-net?'

'No good. It would be too smart for us. I tell you, Saunders, it can cover the ground far faster than I can walk. But I think I see how we can manage it. The two books at the end of the shelf are big ones, that go right back against the wall. The others are very thin. I'll take out one at a time, and you slide the rest along, until we have it squashed between the end two.'

It certainly seemed to be the best plan. One by one as they took out the books, the space behind grew smaller and smaller. There was something in it that was certainly very much alive.

Once they caught sight of fingers feeling for a way of escape. At last they had it pressed between the two big books.

'There's muscle there, if there isn't warm flesh and blood,' said Saunders, as he held them together. 'It seems to be a hand right enough, too. I suppose this is a sort of infectious hallucination. I've read about such cases before.'

'Infectious fiddlesticks!' said Eustace, his face white with anger; 'bring the thing downstairs. We'll get it back into the box.'

It was not altogether easy, but they were successful at last. 'Drive in the screws,' said Eustace; 'we won't run any risks. Put the box in this old desk of mine. There's nothing in it that I want. Here's the key. Thank goodness there's nothing wrong with the lock.'

'Quite a lively evening,' said Saunders. 'Now let's hear more about your uncle.'

They sat up together until early morning. Saunders had no desire for sleep. Eustace was trying to explain and to forget; to conceal from himself a fear that he had never felt before—the fear of walking alone down the long corridor to his bedroom.

'Whatever it was,' said Eustace to Saunders on the following morning, 'I propose that we drop the subject. There's nothing to keep us here for the next ten days. We'll motor up to the Lakes and get some climbing.'

'And see nobody all day, and sit bored to death with each other every night. Not for me, thanks. Why not run up to town? Run's the exact word in this case, isn't it? We're both in such a blessed funk. Pull yourself together, Eustace, and let's have another look at the hand.'

'As you like,' said Eustace; 'there's the key.'

They went into the library and opened the desk. The box was as they had left it on the previous night.

'What are you waiting for?' asked Eustace.

'I am waiting for you to volunteer to open the lid. However since you seem to funk it, allow me. There doesn't seem to be the likelihood of any rumpus this morning at all events.' He opened the lid and picked out the hand.

'Cold?' asked Eustace.

'Tepid. A bit below blood heat by the feel. Soft and supple too. If it's the embalming, it's a sort of embalming I've never seen before. Is it your uncle's hand?'

'Oh yes, it's his all right,' said Eustace. 'I should know those long thin fingers anywhere. Put it back in the box, Saunders. Never mind about the screws. I'll lock the desk, so that there'll be no chance of its getting out. We'll compromise by motoring up to town for a week. If we can get off soon after lunch, we ought to be at Grantham or Stamford by night.'

'Right,' said Saunders, 'and tomorrow—oh, well, by tomorrow we shall have forgotten all about this beastly thing.'

If, when the morrow came, they had not forgotten, it was certainly true that at the end of the week they were able to tell a very vivid ghost-story at the little supper Eustace gave on Halloween.

'You don't want us to believe that it's true, Mr Borlsover? How perfectly awful!'

'I'll take my oath on it, and so would Saunders here; wouldn't you, old chap?'

'Any number of oaths,' said Saunders. 'It was a long thin hand, you know, and it gripped me just like that.'

'Don't, Mr Saunders! Don't! How perfectly horrid! Now tell us another one, do! Only a really creepy one, please.'

'Here's a pretty mess!' said Eustace on the following day, as he threw a letter across the table to Saunders. 'It's your affair, though. Mrs Merrit, if I understand it, gives a month's notice.'

'Oh, that's quite absurd on Mrs Merrit's part,' replied

Saunders. 'She doesn't know what she's talking about. Let's see what she says.'

> Dear Sir [he read]. This is to let you know that I must give you a month's notice as from Tuesday, the 13th. For a long time I've felt the place too big for me; but when Jane Parfit and Emma Laidlaw go off with scarcely as much as an "If you please", after frightening the wits out of the other girls, so that they can't turn out a room by themselves or walk alone down the stairs for fear of treading on half-frozen toads or hearing it run along the passages at night, all I can say is that it's no place for me. So I must ask you, Mr Borlsover, sir, to find a new housekeeper, that has no objection to large and lonely houses, which some people do say, not that I believe them for a minute, my poor mother always having been a Wesleyan, are haunted.
>
> Yours faithfully,
>
> Elizabeth Merrit.
>
> PS.—I should be obliged if you would give my respects to Mr Saunders. I hope that he won't run any risks with his cold.

'Saunders,' said Eustace, 'you've always had a wonderful way with you in dealing with servants. You mustn't let poor old Merrit go.'

'Of course she shan't go,' said Saunders. 'She's probably only angling for a rise in salary. I'll write to her this morning.'

'No. There's nothing like a personal interview. We've had enough of town. We'll go back tomorrow, and you must work your cold for all it's worth. Don't forget that it's got on to the chest, and will require weeks of feeding up and nursing.'

'All right; I think I can manage Mrs Merrit.'

But Mrs Merrit was more obstinate than he had thought. She was very sorry to hear of Mr Saunders's cold, and how he lay awake all night in London coughing; very sorry indeed. She'd change his room for him, gladly, and get the south room aired, and wouldn't he have a hot basin of bread and milk last thing at night? But she was afraid that she would have to leave at the end of the month.

'Try her with an increase of salary,' was the advice of Eustace.

It was no use. Mrs Merrit was obdurate, though she knew of a Mrs Goddard, who had been housekeeper to Lord Gargrave, who might be glad to come at the salary mentioned.

'What's the matter with the servants, Morton?' asked Eustace that evening, when he brought the coffee into the library. 'What's all this about Mrs Merrit wanting to leave?'

'If you please, sir, I was going to mention it myself. I have a confession to make, sir. When I found your note, asking me to open that desk and take out the box with the rat, I broke the lock, as you told me, and was glad to do it, because I could hear the animal in the box making a great noise, and I thought it wanted food. So I took out the box, sir, and got a cage, and was going to transfer it, when the animal got away.'

'What in the world are you talking about? I never wrote any such note.'

'Excuse me, sir; it was the note I picked up here on the floor on the day you and Mr Saunders left. I have it in my pocket now.'

It certainly seemed to be in Eustace's handwriting. It was written in pencil, and began somewhat abruptly.

'Get a hammer, Morton,' he read, 'or some other tool and break open the lock in the old desk in the library. Take out the box that is inside. You need not do anything else. The lid is already open. Eustace Borlsover.'

'And you opened the desk?'

'Yes, sir; and, as I was getting the cage ready, the animal hopped out.'

'What animal?'

'The animal inside the box, sir.'

'What did it look like?'

'Well, sir, I couldn't tell you,' said Morton nervously. 'My back was turned, and it was halfway down the room when I looked up.'

'What was its colour?' asked Saunders. 'Black?'

'Oh no, sir; a greyish white. It crept along in a very funny way, sir. I don't think it had a tail.'

'What did you do then?'

'I tried to catch it; but it was no use. So I set the rat-traps and kept the library shut. Then that girl, Emma Laidlaw, left the door open when she was cleaning, and I think it must have escaped.'

'And you think it is the animal that's been frightening the maids?'

'Well, no sir, not quite. They said it was—you'll excuse me sir—a hand that they saw. Emma trod on it once at the bottom of the stairs. She thought then it was a half-frozen toad, only white. And then Parfit was washing up the dishes in the scullery. She wasn't thinking about anything in particular. It was close on dusk. She took her hands out of the water and was drying them absent-minded like on the roller towel, when she found she was drying someone else's hand as well, only colder than hers.'

'What nonsense!' exclaimed Saunders.

'Exactly sir; that's what I told her; but we couldn't get her to stop.'

'You don't believe all this?' said Eustace, turning suddenly towards the butler.

'Me, sir? Oh no, sir! I've not seen anything.'

'Nor heard anything?'

'Well, sir, if you must know, the bells do ring at odd times, and there's nobody there when we go; and when we go round to draw the blinds of a night, as often as not somebody's been there before us. But, as I says to Mrs Merrit, a young monkey might do wonderful things, and we all know that Mr Borlsover has had some strange animals about the place.'

'Very well, Morton, that will do.'

'What do you make of it?' asked Saunders, when they were alone. 'I mean of the letter he said you wrote.'

'Oh, that's simple enough,' said Eustace. 'See the paper it's written on? I stopped using that paper years ago, but there were a few odd sheets and envelopes left in the old desk. We never fastened up the lid of the box before locking it in. The hand got out, found a pencil, wrote this note, and shoved it through the crack on to the floor, where Morton found it. That's plain as daylight.'

'But the hand couldn't write!'

'Couldn't it? You've not seen it do the things I've seen.'

And he told Saunders more of what had happened at Eastbourne.

'Well,' said Saunders, 'in that case we have at least an explanation of the legacy. It was the hand which wrote, unknown to your uncle, that letter to your solicitor bequeathing itself to you. Your uncle had no more to do with that request than I. In fact, it would seem that he had some idea of this automatic writing and feared it.'

'Then if it's not my uncle, what is it?'

'I suppose some people might say that a disembodied spirit

had got your uncle to educate and prepare a little body for it. Now it's got into that little body and is off on its own.'

'Well, what are we to do?'

'We'll keep our eyes open,' said Saunders, 'and try to catch it. If we can't do that, we shall have to wait till the bally clockwork runs down. After all, if it's flesh and blood, it can't live forever.'

For two days nothing happened. Then Saunders saw it sliding down the banister in the hall. He was taken unawares and lost a full second before he started in pursuit, only to find that the thing had escaped him. Three days later Eustace, writing alone in the library at night, saw it sitting on an open book at the other end of the room. The fingers crept over the page, as if it were reading; but before he had time to get up from his seat, it had taken the alarm, and was pulling itself up the curtains. Eustace watched it grimly, as it hung on to the cornice with three fingers and flicked thumb and forefinger at him in an expression of scornful derisio.

'I know what I'll do,' he said. 'If I only get it into the open I'll set the dogs on to it.'

He spoke to Saunders of the suggestion.

'It's a jolly good idea,' he said; 'only we won't wait till we find it out of doors. We'll get the dogs. There are the two terriers and the under-keeper's Irish mongrel, that's on to rats like a flash. Yom-spaniel has not got spirit enough for this sort of game.'

They brought the dogs into the house, and the keeper's Irish mongrel chewed up the slippers, and the terriers tripped up Morton as he waited at table; but all three were welcome. Even false security is better than no security at all.

For a fortnight nothing happened. Then the hand was caught not by the dogs, but by Mrs Merrit's grey parrot. The bird was in the habit of periodically removing the pins that kept its seed-

and water-tin in place, and of escaping through the holes in the side of the cage. When once at liberty, Peter would show no inclination to return, and would often be about the house for days. Now, after six consecutive weeks of captivity, Peter had again discovered a new way of unloosing his bolts and was, at large, exploring the tapestried forests of the curtains and singing songs in praise of liberty from cornice and picture rail.

'It's no use your trying to catch him,' said Eustace to Mrs Merrit, as she came into the study one afternoon towards dusk with a step-ladder. 'You'd much better leave Peter alone. Starve him into surrender, Mrs Merrit; and don't leave bananas and seed about for him to peck at when he fancies he's hungry. You're far too soft-hearted.'

'Well, sir, I see he's right out of reach now on that picture-rail; so if you wouldn't mind closing the door, sir, when you leave the room, I'll bring his cage in tonight and put some meat inside it. He's that fond of meat, though it does make him pull out his feathers to suck the quills. They *do* say that if you cook—'

'Never mind, Mrs Merrit,' said Eustace, who was busy writing; 'that will do; I'll keep an eye on the bird.'

For a short time there was silence in the room.

'Scratch poor Peter,' said the bird. 'Scratch poor old Peter!'

'Be quiet, you beastly bird!'

'Poor old Peter! Scratch poor Peter; do!'

'I'm more likely to wring your neck, if I get hold of you.' He looked up at the picture-rail, and there was the hand, holding on to a hook with three fingers, and slowly scratching the head of the parrot with the fourth. Eustace ran to the bell and pressed it hard; then across to the window, which he closed with a bang. Frightened by the noise, the parrot shook its wings preparatory to flight, and, as it did so, the fingers of the hand got hold of it by the throat. There was a shrill scream from Peter, as he fluttered across the room, wheeling round in circles that ever descended, borne down under the weight that clung to him. The bird dropped at last quite suddenly, and Eustace saw fingers and feathers rolled into an inextricable mass on the floor. The struggle abruptly ceased, as finger and thumb squeezed the neck; the bird's eyes rolled up to show the white, and there was a faint, half-choked gurgle. But, before the fingers had time to loose their hold, Eustace had them in his own.

'Send Mr Saunders here at once,' he said to the maid who came in answer to the bell. 'Tell him I want him immediately.'

Then he went with the hand to the fire. There was a ragged gash across the back, where the bird's beak had torn it, but no blood oozed from the wound. He noted with disgust that the nails had grown long and discoloured.

'I'll burn the beastly thing,' he said. But he could not burn it. He tried to throw it into the flames, but his own hands, as if impelled by some old primitive feeling, would not let him. And so Saunders found him, pale and irresolute, with the hand still clasped tightly in his fingers.

'I've got it at last,' he said, in a tone of triumph.

'Good, let's have a look at it.'

'Not when it's loose. Get me some nails and a hammer and a board of some sort.'

'Can you hold it all right?'

'Yes, the thing's quite limp; tired out with throttling poor old Peter, I should say.'

'And now,' said Saunders, when he returned with the things, 'what are we going to do?'

'Drive a nail through it first, so that it can't get away. Then we can take our time over examining it.'

'Do it yourself,' said Saunders. 'I don't mind helping you with guinea-pigs occasionally, when there's something to be learned, partly because I don't fear a guinea-pig's revenge. This thing's different.'

'Oh, my aunt!' he giggled hysterically, 'look at it now.' For the hand was writhing in agonized contortions, squirming and wriggling upon the nail like a worm upon the hook.

'Well,' said Saunders, 'you've done it now. I'll leave you to examine it.'

'Don't go, in heaven's name! Cover it up, man; cover it up! Shove a cloth over it! Here!' and he pulled off the antimacassar from the back of a chair and wrapped the board in it. 'Now get the keys from my pocket and open the safe. Chuck the other things out. Oh, Lord, it's getting itself into frightful knots! Open it quick!' He threw the thing in and banged the door.

'We'll keep it there till it dies,' he said. 'May I burn in hell, if I ever open the door of that safe again.'

Mrs Merrit departed at the end of the month. Her successor, Mrs Handyside, certainly was more successful in the management of the servants. Early in her rule she declared that she would stand no nonsense, and gossip soon withered and died.

'I shouldn't be surprised if Eustace married one of these days,' said Saunders. 'Well, I'm in no hurry for such an event. I know him far too well for the future Mrs Borlsover to like me. It will be the same old story again; a long friendship slowly made—marriage—and a long friendship quickly forgotten.'

But Eustace did not follow the advice of his uncle and marry. Old habits crept over and covered his new experience. He was, if anything, less morose, and showed a great inclination to take his natural part in country society.

Then came the burglary. The man, it was said, broke into the house by way of the conservatory. It was really little more than an attempt, for they only succeeded in carrying away a few pieces of plate from the pantry. The safe in the study was certainly found open and empty, but, as Mr Borlsover informed the police inspector, he had kept nothing of value in it during the last six months.

'Then you're lucky in getting off so easily, sir,' the man replied. 'By the way they have gone about their business I should say the were experienced cracksmen. They must have caught the alarm when they were just beginning their evening's work.'

'Yes,' said Eustace, 'I suppose I am lucky.'

'I've no doubt,' said the inspector, 'that we shall be able to trace the men. I've said that they must have been old hands at the game. The way they got in and opened the safe shows that. But there's one little thing that puzzles me. One of them was careless enough not to wear gloves, and I'm bothered if I know what he was trying to do. I've traced his finger-marks on the new varnish on the window-sashes in every one of the downstairs rooms. They are very distinctive ones too.'

'Right hand or left or both?' asked Eustace.

'Oh, right every time. That's the funny thing. He must have been a foolhardy fellow, and I rather think it was him that wrote that.' He took out a slip of paper from his pocket. 'That's what he wrote, sir: "I've got out, Eustace Borlsover, but I'll be back before long." Some jailbird just escaped, I suppose. It will make it all the easier for us to trace him. Do you know the writing, sir?'

'No,' said Eustace. 'It's not the writing of anyone I know.'

'I'm not going to stay here any longer,' said Eustace to Saunders at luncheon. 'I've got on far better during the last six months than I expected, but I'm not going to run the risk of seeing that thing again. I shall go up to town this afternoon. Get Morton to put my things together, and join me with the car at Brighton on the day after tomorrow. And bring the proofs of those two papers with you. We'll run over them together.'

'How long are you going to be away?'

'I can't say for certain, but be prepared to stay for some time. We've stuck to work pretty closely through the summer, and I for one need a holiday. I'll engage the rooms at Brighton. You'll find it best to break the journey at Hitchin. I'll wire to you there at the "Crown" to tell you the Brighton address.'

The house he chose at Brighton was in a terrace. He had been there before. It was kept by his old college gyp, a man of discreet silence, who was admirably partnered by an excellent cook. The rooms were on the first floor. The two bedrooms were at the back, and opened out of each other. 'Mr Saunders can have the smaller one, though it is the only one with a fire-place,' he said. 'I'll stick to the larger of the two, since it's got a bathroom adjoining. I wonder what time he'll arrive with the car.'

Saunders came about seven, cold and cross and dirty. 'We'll light the fire in the dining-room,' said Eustace, 'and get Prince to unpack some of the things while we are at dinner. What were the roads like?'

'Rotten. Swimming with mud, and a beastly cold wind against us all day. And this is July. Dear Old England!'

'Yes,' said Eustace, 'I think we might do worse than leave Old England for a few months.'

They turned in soon after twelve.

'You oughtn't to feel cold, Saunders,' said Eustace, 'when you can afford to sport a great fur-lined coat like this. 'You do yourself very well, all things considered. Look at those gloves, for instance. Who could possibly feel cold when wearing them?'

'They are far too clumsy, though, for driving. Try them on and see,' and he tossed them through the door on to Eustace's bed and went on with his unpacking. A minute later he heard a shrill cry of terror. 'Oh, Lord,' he heard, 'it's in the glove! Quick, Saunders quick!' Then came a smacking thud. Eustace had thrown it from him. 'I've chucked it into the bathroom,' he gasped; 'it's hit the wall and fallen into the bath. Come now, if you want to help,' Saunders, with a lighted candle in his hand, looked over the edge of the bath. There it was, old and maimed, dumb and blind, with a ragged hole in the middle, crawling, staggering, trying to creep up the slippery sides, only to fall back helpless.

'Stay there,' said Saunders. 'I'll empty a collar-box or something and we'll jam it in. It can't get out while I'm away.'

'Yes, it can,' shouted Eustace. 'It's getting out now; it's climbing up the plug-chain.—No, you brute, you filthy brute, you don't!—Come back, Saunders; it's getting away from me. I can't hold it; it's all slippery. Curse its claws! Shut the window, you idiot! It's got out!' There was the sound of something dropping on to the hard flag-stones below, and Eustace fell back fainting.

For a fortnight he was ill.

'I don't know what to make of it,' the doctor said to Saunders. 'I can only suppose that Mr Borlsover has suffered some great emotional shock. You had better let me send someone to help you nurse him. And by all means indulge that whim of his never to be left alone in the dark. I would keep a light burning all night, if I were you. But he *must* have more fresh air. It's perfectly absurd, this hatred of open windows.'

Eustace would have no one with him but Saunders. 'I don't want the other man,' he said. 'They'd smuggle it in somehow. I know they would.'

'Don't worry about it, old chap. This sort of thing can't go on indefinitely. You know I saw it this time as well as you. It wasn't half so active. It won't go on living much longer, especially after that fall. I heard it hit the flags myself. As soon as you're a bit stronger, we'll leave this place, not bag and baggage, but with only the clothes on our backs, so that it won't be able to hide anywhere. We'll escape it that way. We won't give any address, and we won't have any parcels sent after us. Cheer up, Eustace! You'll be well-enough to leave in a day or two. The doctor says I can take you out in a chair tomorrow.'

'What have I done?' asked Eustace. 'Why does it come after me? I'm no worse than other men. I'm no worse than you, Saunders; you know I'm not. It was you who was at the bottom of that dirty business in San Diego, and that was fifteen years ago.'

'It's not that, of course,' said Saunders. 'We are in the twentieth century, and even the parsons have dropped the idea of your old sins finding you out. Before you caught the hand in the library, it was filled with pure malevolence—to you and all mankind. After you spiked it through with that nail, it naturally forgot about other people and concentrated its attention on you. It was shut up in that safe, you know, for nearly six months. That gives plenty of time for thinking of revenge.'

Eustace Borlsover would not leave his room, but he thought there might be something in Saunders's suggestion of a sudden departure from Brighton. He began rapidly to regain his strength.

'We'll go on the first of September,' he said.

The evening of the thirty-first of August was oppressively warm. Though at midday the windows had been wide open, they had been shut an hour or so before dusk. Mrs Prince had long since ceased to wonder at the strange habits of the gentlemen on the first floor. Soon after their arrival she had been told to take down the heavy window curtains in the two bedrooms, and day by day the rooms had seemed to grow more bare. Nothing was left lying about.

'Mr Borlsover doesn't like to have any place where dirt can collect,' Saunders had said as an excuse. 'He likes to see into all the corners of the room.'

'Couldn't I open the window just a little?' he said to Eustace that evening. 'We're simply roasting in here, you know.'

'No, leave well alone. We're not a couple of boarding-school misses fresh from a course of hygiene lectures. Get the chessboard out.'

They sat down and played. At ten o'clock Mrs Prince came to the door with a note. 'I am sorry I didn't bring it before,' she said, 'but it was left in the letter-box.'

'Open it, Saunders, and see if it wants answering.'

It was very brief. There was neither address nor signature.

'Will eleven o'clock tonight be suitable for our last appointment?'

'Who is it from?' asked Borlsover.

'It was meant for me,' said Saunders. 'There's no answer, Mrs Prince,' and he put the paper into his pocket.

'A dunning letter from a tailor; I suppose he must have got wind of our leaving.'

It was a clever lie, and Eustace asked no more questions. They went on with their game.

On the landing outside Saunders could hear the grandfather's clock whispering the seconds, blurting out the quarter-hours.

'Check,' said Eustace. The clock struck eleven. At the same time there was a gentle knocking on the door; it seemed to come from the bottom panel.

'Who's there?' asked Eustace.

There was no answer.

'Mrs Prince, is that you?'

'She is up above,' said Saunders; 'I can hear her walking

about the room.'

'Then lock the door; bolt it too. Your move, Saunders.'

While Saunders sat with his eyes on the chess-board, Eustace walked over to the window and examined the fastenings. He did the same in Saunders's room, and the bathroom. There were no doors between the three rooms, or he would have shut and locked them too.

'Now, Saunders,' he said, 'don't stay all night over your move. I've had time to smoke one cigarette already. It's bad to keep an invalid waiting. There's only one possible thing for you to do. What was that?'

'The ivy blowing against the window. There, it's your move now, Eustace.'

'It wasn't the ivy, you idiot! It was someone tapping at the window,' and he pulled up the blind. On the outer side of the window, clinging to the sash, was the hand.

'What is it that it's holding?'

'It's a pocket-knife. It's going to try to open the window by pushing back the fastener with the blade.'

'Well, let it try,' said Eustace. 'Those fasteners screw down; they can't be opened that way. Anyhow, we'll close the shutters. It's your move, Saunders; I've played.'

But Saunders found it impossible to fix his attention on the game. He could not understand Eustace, who seemed all at once to have lost his fear. 'What do you say to some wine?' he asked. 'You seem to be taking things coolly, but I don't mind confessing that I'm in a blessed funk.'

'You've no need to be. There's nothing supernatural about that hand, Saunders. I mean it seems to be governed by the laws of time and space. It's not the sort of thing that vanishes into thin air or slides through oaken doors. And since that's so, I defy it to get in here. We'll leave the place in the morning. I for one have bottomed the depths of fear. Fill your glass, man! The windows are all shuttered; the door is locked and bolted. Pledge me my Uncle Adrian! Drink, man! What are you waiting for?'

Saunders was standing with his glass half raised. 'It can get in,' he said hoarsely; 'it can get in. We've forgotten. There's the fireplace in my bedroom. It will come down the chimney.'

'Quick!' said Eustace, as he rushed into the other room; 'we haven't a minute to lose. What can we do? Light the fire, Saunders. Give me a match, quick!'

'They must be all in the other room. I'll get them.'

'Hurry, man, for goodness' sake! Look in the bookcase! Look in the bathroom! Here, come and stand here; I'll look.'

'Be quick!' shouted Saunders. 'I can hear something!'

'Then plug a sheet from your bed up the chimney. No, here's a match!' He had found one at last that had slipped into a crack in the floor.

'Is the fire laid? Good, but it may not burn. I know—the oil from that old reading-lamp and this cotton-wool. Now the match, quick! Pull the sheet away, you fool! We don't want it now.'

There was a great roar from the grate, as the flames shot up. Saunders had been a fraction of a second too late with the sheet. The oil had fallen on to it. It, too, was burning.

'The whole place will be on fire!' cried Eustace, as he tried to beat out the flames with a blanket. 'It's no good! I can't manage it. You must open the door, Saunders, and get help.'

Saunders ran to the door and fumbled with the bolts. The key was stiff in the lock. 'Hurry,' shouted Eustace, 'or the heat will be too much for me.' The key turned in the lock at last. For half a second Saunders stopped to look back. Afterwards he could never be quite sure as to what he had seen, but at the time he thought that something black and charred was creeping slowly, very slowly, from the mass of flames towards Eustace Borlsover. For a moment he thought of returning to his friend; but the noise and the smell of the burning sent him running down the passage, crying: 'Fire! Fire!' He rushed to the telephone to summon help, and then back to the bathroom—he should have thought of that before—for water. As he burst into the bedroom there came a scream of terror which ended suddenly, and then the sound of a heavy fall.

This is the story which I heard on successive Saturday evenings from the senior mathematical master at a second-rate suburban school. For Saunders has had to earn a living in a way which other men might reckon less congenial than his old manner of life. I had mentioned by chance the name of Adrian Borlsover, and wondered at the time why he changed the conversation with such unusual abruptness. A week later Saunders began to tell me something of his own history; sordid enough, though shielded with a reserve I could well understand, for it had to cover not only his failings, but those of a dead friend. Of the final tragedy he was at first especially loath to speak; and it was only gradually that I was able to piece together the narrative of the preceding pages. Saunders was reluctant to draw any conclusions. At one time he thought that the fingered beast had been animated by the spirit of Sigismund Borlsover, a sinister eighteenth-century ancestor, who, according to legend, built and worshipped in the ugly pagan temple that overlooked the lake. At another time Saunders believed the spirit to belong to a man whom Eustace had once employed as a laboratory assistant, 'a black-haired, spiteful little brute,' he said, 'who died cursing his doctor, because the fellow couldn't help him to live to settle some paltry score with Borlsover.'

From the point of view of direct contemporary evidence, Saunders's story is practically uncorroborated. All the letters mentioned in the narrative were destroyed, with the exception of the last note which Eustace received, or rather which he would have received, had not Saunders intercepted it. That I have seen myself. The handwriting was thin and shaky, the handwriting of an old man. I remember the Greek V was used in 'appointment'. A little thing that amused me at the time was that Saunders seemed to keep the note pressed between the pages of his Bible.

I had seen Adrian Borlsover once. Saunders I learnt to know well. It was by chance, however, and not by design, that I met a third person of the story, Morton, the butler. Saunders and I were walking in the Zoological Gardens one Sunday afternoon, when he called my attention to an old man who was standing before the door of the Reptile House.

'Why, Morton,' he said, clapping him on the back, 'how is the world treating you?'

'Poorly, Mr Saunders,' said the old fellow, though his face lighted up at the greeting. 'The winters drag terribly nowadays. There don't seem no summers or springs.'

'You haven't found what you were looking for, I suppose?'

'No, sir, not yet; but I shall some day. I always told them that Mr Borlsover kept some queer animals.'

'And what is he looking for?' I asked, when we had parted from him.

'A beast with five fingers,' said Saunders. 'This afternoon, since he has been in the Reptile House, I suppose it will be a reptile with a hand. Next week it will be a monkey with practically no body. The poor old chap is a born materialist.'

BOOMERANG

Oscar Cook

Warwick threw himself into a chair beside me, hitched up his trousers, and, leaning across, tapped me on the knee. 'You remember the story about Mendingham which you told me?' he asked.

I nodded. I was not likely to forget that affair. 'Well,' he went on, 'I've got as good a one to tell you. Had it straight from the filly's mouth, so to speak—and it's red-hot.'

I edged away in my chair, for there was something positively ghoulish in his delight, in the coarse way by which he referred to a woman, and one who, if my inference were correct, must have known tragedy. But there is no stopping Warwick: he knows or admits no finer feelings or shame when his thirst for 'copy' is aroused. Like the little boy in the well-known picture, 'he won't be happy till he's "quenched" it'.

I ordered drinks, and when they had been served and we were alone, bade him get on with his sordid story.

'It's a wild tale,' he began, 'of two planter fellows in the interior of Borneo—and, as usual, there's a woman.'

'*The* woman?' I could not refrain from asking, thinking of his earlier remark.

'The same,' he replied. 'A veritable golden-haired filly, only her mane is streaked with grey and there's a great livid scar or weal right round her neck. She's the wife of Leopold Thring. The other end of the triangle is Clifford Macy'

'And where do you come in?' I inquired.

Warwick closed one eye and pursed his lips.

'As a spinner of yarns,' he answered sententiously. Then, with a return to his usual cynicism, 'The filly is down and out, but for some silly religious scruples feels she must live. I bought the story, therefore, after verifying the facts. Shall I go on?'

I nodded, for I must admit I was genuinely interested. The eternal triangle always intrigues: set in the wilds of Borneo it promised a variation of incident unusually refreshing in these sophisticated days. Besides, that scar was eloquent.

Warwick chuckled.

'The two men were partners,' he went on, 'on a small experimental estate far up in the interior. They had been at it for six years and were just about to reap the fruits of their labours very handsomely. Incidentally, Macy had been out in the Colony the full six years—and the strain was beginning to tell. Thring had been home eighteen months before, and on coming back had brought his bride, Rhona.

'That was the beginning of the trouble. It split up the partnership; brought in a new element: meant the building of a new bungalow.'

'For Macy?' I asked.

'Yes. And he didn't take kindly to it. He had got set. And then there was the loneliness of night after night alone, while the others—you understand?'

I nodded.

'Well,' Warwick continued, 'the expected happened. Macy flirted, philandered, and then fell violently in love. He was one of those fellows who never did things by halves. If he drank, he'd get fighting drunk: if he loved, he went all out on it: if he hated—well, hell was let loose.'

'And—Mrs Thring?' I queried, for it seemed to me that she might have a point of view.

'Fell between two stools—as so many women of a certain type do. She began by being just friendly and kind—you know the sort of thing—cheering the lonely man up, drifted into woman's eternal game of flirting, and then began to grow a little afraid of the fire she'd kindled. Too late she realized that she couldn't put the fire out—either hers or Macy's—and all the while she clung to some hereditary religious scruples.

'Thring was in many ways easy-going, but at the same time possessed of a curiously intense strain of jealous possessiveness. He was generous, too. If asked, he would share or give away his last shirt or crust. But let him think or feel that his rights or dues were being curtailed or taken and—well, he was a tough customer of rather primitive ideas.

'Rhona—that's the easiest way to think of the filly—soon found she was playing a game beyond her powers. Hers was no poker face, and Thring began to sense that something was wrong. She couldn't dissemble, and Macy made no attempt to hide his feelings. He didn't make it easy for her, and I guess from what the girl told me, life about this time was for her a sort of glorified hell—a suspicious husband on one hand, and an impetuous, devil-may-care lover on the other. She was living on a volcano.'

'Which might explode any minute.' I quietly said.

Warwick nodded.

'Exactly; or whenever Thring chose to spring the mine. He held the key to the situation, or, should I say, the time-fuse? The old story, but set in a primitive land full of possibilities.

You've got me?'

For answer I offered Warwick a cigarette, and, taking one myself lighted both.

'So far,' I said, 'with all your journalistic skill you've not got off the beaten track. Can't you improve?'

He chuckled, blew a cloud of smoke, and once again tapped my knee in his irritating manner.

'Your cynicism,' he countered, 'is but a poor cloak for your curiosity. In reality you're jumping mad to know the end, eh?'

I made no reply, and he went on.

'Well, matters went on from day to day till Rhona became worn to the proverbial shadow. Thring wanted to send her home, but she wouldn't go. She owed a duty to her husband: she couldn't bear to be parted from her lover, and she didn't dare leave the two men alone. She was terribly, horribly afraid.

'Macy grew more and more openly amorous and less restrained. Thring watched whenever possible with the cunning of an iguana. Then came a rainy, damp spell that tried the nerves to the uttermost and the inevitable stupid little disagreements between Rhona and Thring—mere trifles, but enough to let the lid off. He challenged her—'

'And she?' I could not help asking, for Warwick has, I must admit, the knack of keeping one on edge.

'Like a blithering but sublime little idiot admitted that it was all true.'

For nearly a minute I was speechless. Somehow, although underneath I had expected Rhona to behave so, it seemed such a senseless, unbelievable thing to do. Then at last I found my voice.

'And Thring?' I said simply.

Warwick emptied his glass at a gulp.

'That's the most curious thing in the whole yarn,' he

answered slowly 'Thring took it as quietly as a lamb.'

'Stunned?' I suggested.

'That's what Rhona thought: what Macy believed when Rhona told him what had happened. In reality he must have been burning mad, a mass of white-hot revenge controlled by a devilish, cunning brain: he waited. A scene or a fight—and Macy was a big man—would have done no good. He would get his own back in his own time and in his own way. Meanwhile, there was the lull before the storm.

'Then, as so often happens, fate played a hand. Macy went sick with malaria—really ill—and even Thring had to admit the necessity for Rhona to nurse him practically night and day. Macy owned his eventual recovery to her care, but even so his convalescence was a long job. In the end Rhona, too, crocked up through overwork, and Thring had them both on his hands. This was an opportunity better than he could have planned—it separated the lovers and gave him complete control.

'Obviously the time was ripe, ripe for Thring to score his revenge. The rains were over, the jungle had ceased wintering, and spring was in the air. The young grass and vegetation were shooting into new life: concurrently all the creepy, crawly insect life of the jungle and estate was young and vigorous and hungry, too. These facts gave Thring the germ of an idea which he was not slow to perfect—an idea as devilish as man could devise.'

Warwick paused to press out the stub of his cigarette, and noticing that even he seemed affected by his recital, I prepared myself as best I could for a really gruesome horror. All I said however, was, 'Go on.'

'It seems,' he continued, 'that in Borneo there is a kind of mammoth earwig—a thing almost as fine and gossamer as a spider's web, as long as a good-sized caterpillar, that lives on waxy secretions. These are integral parts of some flowers and trees, and lie buried deep in their recesses. It is one of the terrors of these particular tropics, for it moves and rests so lightly on a human being that one is practically unconscious of it, while, like its English relation, it has a decided liking for the human ear: on account of man's carnivorous diet the wax in this has a strong and very succulent taste.'

As Warwick gave me those details, he sat upright on the edge of his easy-chair. He spoke slowly, emphasizing each point by hitting the palm of his left hand with the clenched first of his right. It was impossible not to see the drift and inference of his remarks.

'You mean?' I began.

'Exactly,' he broke in quickly, blowing a cloud of smoke from a fresh cigarette which he had nervously lighted. 'Exactly. It was a devilish idea. To put the giant earwig on Macy's hair just above the ear.'

'And then...?' I knew the fatuousness of the question, but speech relieved the growing sense of ticklish horror that was creeping over me.

'Do nothing. But rely on the filthy insect running true to type. Once in Macy's ear, it was a thousand-to-one chance against it ever coming out the same way: it would not be able to turn: to back out would be almost an impossibility, and so, feeding as it went, it would crawl right across inside his head, with the result that—'

The picture Warwick was drawing was more than I could bear: even my imagination, dulled by years of legal dry-as-dust affairs, saw and sickened at the possibilities. I put out a hand and gripped Warwick's arm.

'Stop, man!' I cried hoarsely 'For god's sake, don't say any more. I understand. My god, but the man Thring must be a fiend!'

Warwick looked at me, and I saw that even his face had paled.

'*Was*' he said meaningly. 'Perhaps you're right, perhaps he *was* a fiend. Yet, remember, Macy stole his wife.'

'But a torture like that! The deliberate creation of a living torment that would grow into madness. Warwick, you can't condone that!'

He looked at me for a moment and then slowly spread out his hands.

'Perhaps you're right,' he admitted. 'It was a bit thick, I know. But there's more to come.'

I closed my eyes and wondered if I could think of an excuse for leaving Warwick; but in spite of my real horror, my curiosity won the day.

'Get on with it,' I muttered, and leant back, eyes still shut hands clenched. With teeth gritted together as if I myself were actually suffering the pain of that earwig slowly, daily creeping farther into and eating my brain, I waited.

Warwick was not slow to obey.

'I have told you,' he said, 'that Rhona had to nurse Macy, and even when he was better, though still weak, Thring insisted on her looking after him, though now he himself came more often.

'One afternoon Rhona was in Macy's bungalow alone with him: the house-boy was out. Rhona was on the verandah; Macy was asleep in the bedroom. Dusk was just falling; bats were flying about: the flying foxes, heavy with fruit, were returning home; the inevitable house rats were scurrying about the floors; the lamps had not been lit. An eerie, devastating hour. Rhona dropped some needlework and fought back tears. Then from the bedroom came a shriek: "My head! My ear! Oh, god! My ear! Oh, god! The pain!"

'That was the beginning. The earwig had got well inside.

Rhona rushed in and did all she could. Of course, there was nothing to see. Then for a little while Macy would be quiet because the earwig was quiet, sleeping or gorged. Then the vile tiling would move or feed again, and Macy once more would shriek with the pain.

'And so it went on, day by day. Alternate quiet and alternate pain, each day for Macy, for Rhona a hell of nerve-rending expectancy. Waiting, always waiting for the pain that crept and crawled and twisted and writhed and moved slowly, ever slowly, through and across Macy's brain.'

Warwick paused so long that I was compelled to open my eyes. His face was ghastly. Fortunately I could not see my own.

'And Thring?' I asked.

'Came often each day. Pretended sorrow and served out spurious dope—Rhona found the coloured water afterwards. He cleverly urged that Macy should be carried down to the coast for medical treatment, knowing full well that he was too ill and worn to bear the smallest strain. Then when Macy was an utter wreck, broken completely in mind and body, with hollow, hunted eyes, with ever-twitching fingers, with a body no part of which he could properly control or keep still, the earwig came out—at the other ear.

'As it happened, both Thring and Rhona were present. Macy must have suffered an excruciating pain, followed as usual by a period of quiescence: then, feeling a slight ticklish sensation on his cheek, put up his hand to rub or scratch. His fingers came in contact with the earwig and its fine gossamer hair. Instinct did the rest. You follow?'

My tongue was still too dry to enable me to speak. Instead I nodded, and Warwick went on.

'He naturally was curious and looked to see what he was holding. In an instant he realized. Even Rhona could not be in doubt. The hair was faintly but unmistakably covered here and there with blood, with wax and with grey matter.

'For a moment there was absolute silence between the three. At last Macy spoke.

'"My god!" he just whispered. "Oh, my god! What an escape!"

'Rhona burst into tears. Only Thring kept silent, and that was his mistake. The silence worried Macy, weak though he was. He looked from Rhona to Thring, and at the critical moment Thring could not meet his gaze. The truth was out. With an oath Macy *threw* the insect, now dead from the pressure of his fingers, straight into Thring's face. Then he crumpled up in his chair and sobbed and sobbed till even the chair shook.'

Again Warwick paused till I thought he would never go on. I had heard enough, I'll admit, and yet it seemed to me that at least there should be an epilogue.

'Is that all?' I tentatively asked.

Warwick shook his head.

'Nearly, but not quite,' he said. 'Rhona had ceased weeping and kept her eyes fixed on Thring—she dared not go and comfort Macy now. She saw him examine the dead earwig, having picked it up from the floor to which it had fallen, turn it this way and that, then produce from a pocket a magnifying-glass which he used daily for the inspection and detection of leaf disease on certain of the plants. As she watched, she saw the fear and disappointment leave his face, to be replaced by a look of cunning and evil satisfaction. Then for the first time he spoke.

'"Macy!" he called, in a sharp, loud voice.

'Macy looked up.

'Thring held up the earwig. "This is dead now," he said, "dead. As dead as my friendship for you, you swine of a thief, as dead as my love for that whore who was my wife. It's dead, I tell you, dead, but it's a female. D'you get me? A female, and a female lays eggs, and before it died it—"

'He never finished. His baiting at last roused Macy, endowing him with the strength of madness and despair. With one spring he was at Thring's throat, bearing him down to the ground. Over and over they rolled on the floor, struggling for the possession of the great hunting-knife stuck in Thring's belt. One moment Macy was on top, the next, Thring. Their breath and oaths came in great trembling gasps. They kicked and bit and scratched. And all the while Rhona watched, fascinated and terrified. Then Thring got definitely on top. He had one hand on Macy's throat, both knees on his chest, and with his free hand he was feeling for the knife. In that instant Rhona's religious scruples went by the board. She realized she only loved Macy, that her husband didn't count. She rushed to Macy's help. Thring saw her coming and let drive a blow at her head which almost stunned her. She fell on top of him just as he was whipping out the knife. Its edge caught her neck. The sudden spurt of blood shot into Thring's eyes, and blinded him. It was Macy's last chance. He knew it, and he took it.

'When Rhona came back to consciousness, Thring was dead. Macy was standing beside the body, which was gradually swelling to huge proportions as he worked, weakly but steadily, at the white ant exterminator pump, the nozzle of which was pushed down the dead man's throat.'

Warwick ceased. This last had been a long, unbroken recital, and mechanically he picked up his empty glass as if to drain it. The action brought me back to nearly normal. I rang for the waiter—the knob of the electric bell luckily being just over my head. While waiting, I had time to speak.

'I've heard enough,' I said hurriedly, 'to last me a lifetime. You've made me feel positively sick. But there's just one point.

What happened to Macy? Did he live?'

Warwick nodded.

'That's another strange fact. He still lives. He was tried for the murder of Thring, but there was no real evidence. On the other hand, his story was too tall to be believed, with the result—well, you can guess.'

'A lunatic asylum—for life?' I asked.

Warwick nodded again. Then I followed his glance. A waiter was standing by my chair.

'Two double whisky-and-sodas,' I ordered tersely, and then, with shaking fingers, lighted a cigarette.